game misconduct

Copyright © 2025 by Emily Silver

All rights reserved.

This is a work of fiction. Names, characters, places and incidents are either the product of the author's imagination or are use fictitiously. Any resemblance to actual persons, living or dead, businesses, companies, events or locations is entirely coincidental.

No part of this book may be reproduced in any form or by any electronic or mechanical means, including information storage and retrieval systems, without written permission from the author, except for the use of brief quotations in a book review. For more information, please email the author at Emily@authoremilysilver.com.

NO AI TRAINING: Without in any way limiting the author's [and publisher's] exclusive rights under copyright, any use of this publication to "train" generative artificial intelligence (AI) technologies to generate text is expressly prohibited. The author reserves all rights to license uses of this work for generative AI training and development of machine learning language models.

Cover Design by Emily Silver

Editing by Happily Editing Anns

www.authoremilysilver.com

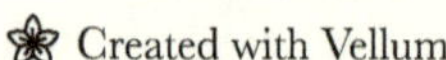 Created with Vellum

GAME MISCONDUCT

A Nashville Knights Novel

EMILY SILVER

Chapter One

HARPER

"I can't read!" Vermilion wails.

Taking a deep breath, I crouch down so I'm on the same level as the seven-year-old. "Why can't you read?"

Tears line Vermilion's eyes.

"My sister took my book last night so I couldn't read. Mommy made her give it back, but I couldn't practice and now I can't read," she tells me through deep, gulping sobs.

"It's okay."

"She told me I don't have to learn to read because the robots are going to do it for us."

"The robots?" I ask. This is something I haven't heard before in all my years of teaching.

Vermilion nods. "Maeve said that the robots are going to do it for us, so I don't have to learn to read and she took my book."

"Does Maeve know how to read?"

She nods.

"Well, until the robots read for us, we need to learn to read."

"But I couldn't practice." Vermilion's chin wobbles.

"Since it's quiet time, why don't you go sit and read before recess so you can practice our new book, okay?"

"I can?"

I nod. "No one is in the beanbag chair, so you get that today."

That lights her up. "Okay!"

She bounds over, red curls springy as she flops into the oversized red chair that lines the ABC-circle rug. She opens her book with a happy smile on her face.

Heading over to my desk, I drop down into my chair and make a note to talk to Vermilion's mom at our fall parent night next week. Having my own older sister, I know how much of a pain they can be. Especially at that age.

Grabbing the stack of papers on my desk, I start to pin them on the bulletin board in the front of the classroom. Every wall in my classroom is covered with a variety of papers. Handprints of the students with what they want to be when they grow up. Pictures of the students playing at recess. Numbers and math problems of the week. Our weekly reading assignment.

I sneak a glance over at Vermilion, and her finger is moving over the page as her mouth says the words to herself.

I smile. This is why I became a teacher—to see kids learning before my eyes.

As chatter starts to rise, I know the students are starting to get antsy to go outside.

Looking at the large clock—used to help the kids tell time—I see it's time for recess. "Okay, everyone. Put your work on your desk. We'll pick it back up when we get back inside."

Happy faces hurry to the door as they line up single file by the cubbies in the room.

Shouts of excitement are loud as I push open the side door to the playground and watch the kids take off on the rubber mulch-covered ground. I take my spot monitoring with the other teachers.

It's the perfect fall day in Nashville. Not too hot, which makes it easy for the kids to burn off some of their energy from sitting all morning. A few fluffy, white clouds float lazily in the sky, but don't provide any shade from the sun.

It's one of the many reasons I love it here and could never seem to leave. These days make everything feel hopeful. Like there are good things coming on the horizon.

"How was your date last night?" Rina asks me. Her eyes aren't on me as she blows the whistle to alert two students to stop fighting over a swing.

"Ugh. Don't ask," I groan. "It was terrible."

"Really?" She turns to face me, shielding her eyes from the sun. "I thought he had so much potential."

I shake my head, watching as a group of students starts playing hopscotch. "He couldn't stop talking about his 401k. Good for you, buddy, for having a retirement account. I do too, but I don't drone on and on about it on a first date."

Rina bumps me with her shoulder. "Sorry, babe. Maybe Michael knows someone else at his office that we can set you up with."

I shake my head. "No. I'm done for a while. I'm tired of first dates."

Exhausted, really.

I thought I was one of the lucky ones and found my soulmate in college. I was wrong. Oh, how wrong I was. But that's not something I like thinking about.

Even if I want a partner, a string of bad first dates makes it hard to want to keep dating.

A foot doctor—who discussed gross foot diseases over dinner.

A self-professed Lego Master—who turned out to be unemployed and living in his parents' basement.

A financial analyst—obsessed with his 401k.

I seem to find the cream of the crop in men.

"Okay." Rina holds up her hands. "What if I find someone that I think is perfect for you? Can I set you up then?"

I waggle my head back and forth in thought. "Maybe."

Rina's smile is triumphant. "That's not a no."

I point a finger in her face. "It's not a yes either."

"You're so stubborn."

I smile at her before turning my attention back to the swings. It's always the point of contention at recess. "You love me for it."

"I don't know why."

Rina is probably one of my closest friends in Nashville. She and her husband, even though they're older than I am, took me under their wing when I first arrived at Nashville Prep.

After everything that happened, I couldn't stay at my old school. I needed a fresh start. Getting an offer to teach at a private school seemed like the best thing at the time. And now I have Rina.

In her late thirties, she's gone prematurely gray and has no interest in coloring her hair. Her hazel eyes are playful, and she never has an unkind word to say about anyone. It's one of the reasons I gravitate toward her and her husband. If I ever need anything, they're there for me.

"How's the house hunting going?" Rina asks, changing the subject.

"I'm looking at a couple next weekend, so fingers crossed. I think one of them might be perfect for me."

"Is it the small bungalow you sent me?"

I nod.

"I don't want to jinx anything, but I think I could get it."

It's really the perfect place for me. A small bungalow on a little piece of land. The housing market in Nashville is hot, so I've been scrimping and saving every penny for the last few years in order to buy my own place. Being that I live a bit outside of the city, it's a little pricier, but I've been watching the bungalow as it's been rehabbed since I started teaching here.

The sage exterior with a dark gray front door calls to me. The interior is open, with hardwood floors and a brand-new kitchen, and it's everything I'd want in my own space.

The owner's suite is in the back of the house, with a sitting room in the front that overlooks a large willow tree. There's even a walkout basement that leads to a nice big yard.

Perfect for a single woman.

Even though I'm far from my California roots, I love it here. I've created my own life.

I have friends that I can call whenever I need them. A good job. A community. Sure, I might be lacking in other areas, but I'm grateful for what I have.

"How about drinks next week after meet-the-teacher night?" Rina asks, checking her watch. "Ugh. I don't want to go inside. I wish we could teach outside today."

"Why don't you?"

I've done it before on good days. It's always nice for a change to get the kids doing something different.

"Math time."

"Say no more."

Checking the time on my own watch, I have to admit that recess is over. The teacher on the opposite side of the playground blows their whistle, and the students start scurrying to line up—haphazard at best.

"Next week?" Rina asks. "No backing out."

"Hey!" I'm indignant. "I don't back out nearly as much as you."

"Yeah, yeah." She rolls her eyes at me. With two young kids, it's understandable.

Counting off my students, I note they're all here and lead the group inside.

"Are we going to read again?" Vermilion asks as I unlock the door and hold it open.

"We're going to read out loud as a class. Do you want to start us off?" I ask her.

Her face beams with pride. "Okay!"

It's quite the change from earlier. Even just a few minutes of practice has helped shift her mood. And hopefully reading out loud will help her gain more confidence in reading.

Teaching might not be the most glamorous job in the world, but I love it. For students like Vermilion. My life might not be what I imagined for myself when I graduated and moved here, but it is what it is.

Even if there's something missing—*someone*, really—I'm happy.

And that's all that matters.

WELCOME
TO
Fabulous
LAS VEGAS
NEVADA

"Dad, will you play chess with me?"

"In a minute, sweetheart. Why don't you ask Sam to play with you until then?"

My words are met with a long-suffering sigh from Sadie. "Because Sam doesn't like chess."

"Chess is boring!" The words are shouted from the back playroom. "Why can't we ever do what I want to do?"

Standing in the kitchen of the open floor plan, I brace myself for what is going to follow. Sending the girls to play together while I tried to get their backpacks ready for school tomorrow didn't last long.

Stomps are followed by Sadie's twin barreling into the kitchen with an attitude that could match an NHL player's.

"We always do what you want to do!" Sadie fires back. "I don't want to play dress-up. I want to play chess!"

"But—" Sam starts. I quickly step between the girls so a fight doesn't break out.

"Okay. Sam, why don't you go play dress-up—"

"I don't want to play dress-up by myself." Sam crosses her arms, staring up at me like it's the dumbest thing in the world. Her caramel-brown hair is pulled back into a messy braid.

Five years since their hair got long enough, and I still can't manage a passable braid to save my life. Bright, blue eyes are full of annoyance. Turning my attention to her identical twin, I'm met with the same look.

"And I don't want to play dress-up, so you have to play by yourself, Sam."

"Dad!" Sam screams, stomping her foot. "Tell her to stop being mean."

I scrub a hand down my face, trying to quell my own rising frustration at the escalating situation. When the two of them entered second grade, it's like their personalities flipped a switch. They became two different people. Two different people that can't seem to get along no matter what I do.

"Then go play in your room, Sam, and Sadie, you can play chess down here."

She quirks a brow at me. "By myself? I can't play chess by myself."

"Can't you be both colors?"

Sadie rolls her eyes at me. "I'll know the moves to do though. I won't learn anything by playing myself."

"You have the book you can use," Sam tells her. "That means you can play by yourself."

"That means you can play by yourself too. Right, Dad?"

Sadie pins me with a stare. No matter how I answer this question, I'm not going to give them an answer that either will like.

Fuck. The problem with raising twin girls. Most days, I'm flying by the seat of my pants and feeling that whatever I do isn't good enough for them.

Maybe if I had someone, it'd be easier. But not just anyone.

There's only one person who could have handled this. But there's no use going down that path right now.

The chime from my phone signals the doorbell. Thank God. Both girls run to the door and peek out the glass on the side windows.

"It's pizza!" Sam yells, excitement now coming from her. At least one girl is happy.

"Why are we having pizza tonight? Isn't pizza for special nights?" Sadie asks.

"Shh!" Sam says. "I want pizza."

"It's not like we're going to return the pizza," I tell them, walking to the door. "I didn't have time to make dinner after practice before the thing at school tonight."

"It's not a thing, Dad. It's fall parent night so you can see everything we've done so far."

I smile at her as I open the door. I fish a large tip out of my wallet and hand it to the delivery guy. Seeing as how I order from them more than I should, they know me. And if I keep giving them good tips, we get pizza faster.

Meaning I keep the girls happy.

"Thanks, man."

"Anytime, Mr. Evans. Thanks for the tip." He jogs down the stairs as I kick the door shut behind me.

Holding the box down, I let them grab the breadsticks and juice boxes from the top and watch as they run into the kitchen and take their seats at the table.

"Gigi will be over in a little bit. I have to go meet with your teachers."

"Why can't Gigi meet our teachers and you stay home with us?" Sam whines.

I set my crust down and lean across the table. "Is there a reason you don't want me to meet your teacher?"

"Sam talks too much in class."

Sadie sucks the last dregs of her juice and earns a scathing glare from Sam.

"I do not! You're always talking."

"Because I'm smart and answer the questions."

"I'm smart too!" Sam says. "Right, Dad?"

"You're both very smart."

Sadie rolls her eyes at me and before she can argue, I cut her with a look to tell her to cool it.

At least she can read that.

Raising twin eight-year-old girls is not what I had in mind at this stage in my life. If one is happy, it's likely the other isn't for some mundane reason.

I held them back from starting school a year to give them more time to learn and adjust. It seemed to help given how smart—and sassy—they can be on any day of the week.

"How about this?" I grab a breadstick, take a bite, and chew. "If I get good reports from your teacher, then you two can pick what I make us for dinner tomorrow, okay?"

That earns me big smiles and cuts any arguing. "Okay!"

"Can we have grilled cheese with apple slices?" Sadie asks.

"Yeah!" Sam agrees. "That's my favorite."

I smile. "You got it. But I better get good reports from Mrs. Gonzalez. I don't want you two to be the trouble-makers of the class."

"We're not, Dad," Sam tells us.

"Promise?"

"Promise," they agree.

A knock sounds from the door, but this time, it's more to signal that they're here than anything else. "Hi!" Mom's voice rings out.

"Gigi!" the girls yell out.

"Uh-uh. Finish dinner."

Mom toes off her shoes and walks into the kitchen.

I stuff the rest of my breadstick in my mouth and stand to give her a hug.

"Did I not teach you any manners?" Mom shakes her head at me as the girls start giggling.

"Apparently not," I say around a mouthful. "But I don't want to be late."

Mom looks down at her watch before dropping kisses on both of the girls' heads. "You know you're running late, right?"

"What? No, I'm not. It doesn't start for another hour."

"No, it ends in an hour."

"Seriously? Shit."

"I thought you were going late," Mom says. "I told you Monday what time it was."

"Well, obviously I forgot." Grabbing a slice, I find my keys and wallet before stepping into my shoes. "Bye, girls. Be good for Gigi."

The last thing I hear as I'm out the door is the argument I thought was over before dinner came. Chess versus dress-up.

My never-ending battle.

Chapter Three

HARPER

"Vermilion just adores you. You're her favorite teacher. Even more than her art teacher."

I smile back at the woman with auburn curls standing in front of me. It's clear that Vermilion is a spitting image of her mother. "She's a bright young girl."

"She's never wanted to learn before, and we have to pull her away from her homework every night now. And thankfully, her sister has stopped stealing her books."

"I'm glad to hear that. Vermilion loves reading."

"And I have you to thank for that."

I shake the woman's hand as she follows her husband over to Vermilion's desk to see the work she's done this year.

I always enjoy our fall parent night. It's intimate, cozy. I smile as the parents loiter about, chatting familiarly with each other. With the night coming to an end, I start putting away the papers in each student's desk for those that forgot to take them.

"Hey." Rina comes into the room as Vermilion's parents wave goodbye. "Dan just called and I have to pick up Laura from the sitter. She's sick and he can't leave his work dinner. Would you mind watching my class for any parents?"

"You know they aren't my students though, right?"

Rina clasps her hands under her chin. "Please? There's only ten minutes left. I doubt anyone will come."

"Fine." I wave her out of my room. "Go. I'll keep an eye on both rooms."

"You're the best." Rina hugs me before rushing out of the room. "I owe you!"

"Yeah, yeah."

Grabbing my lesson planner and my wheelie chair, I drag it to the doorway to sit and keep an eye on both rooms. Student artwork lines the hallway where the two second grade classrooms are. I love that our school is smaller so the classes aren't packed with kids.

A few parents and teachers walk through the halls. I smile at them as they pass, but it's mostly quiet. With the evening winding down, most have already come and gone.

It gives me the time to plan out my lessons without interruption. And without having to take them home to work on them.

Pounding footsteps sound from the hallway behind me.

"Am I too late? Did I miss it?"

That voice. It doesn't matter that it's out of breath and echoing around the room.

The notebook in my hand falls to the floor.

That voice.

His voice. The one that haunts my dreams. Well, nightmares more like it.

The one that told me he loved me more than life itself. Nothing would ever come between us. He promised. *He lied.*

Seven years have passed, and I am still unprepared. My

stomach swooshes and bile rises, and for a moment, I'm frozen.

I spin in my chair toward the voice because I don't think my legs could hold my weight right about now.

There he is.

Marcus Evans.

The man who obliterated my heart. Standing in this hallway in front of me.

"What the fuck?"

MARCUS

"WHAT THE FUCK?"

Holy shit. I haven't heard that voice in seven years.

Seven years.

Harper Smith. The love of my life and my college sweetheart.

And at one point, my wife. Well, supposed wife. Apparently the paperwork never got filed correctly.

"What the fuck *me*? What the fuck you? My daughters are in your class?"

Harper's blue eyes go wide.

"Your daughters?"

"I thought Mrs. Gonzalez was their teacher?"

Harper was never one to hide her emotions. Especially from me.

And right now, I can see every single emotion play out on her face. Shock. Disbelief. Anger. Rage.

Yeah, rage just about sums up the look on her face. If she were spitting fire, I wouldn't be surprised.

Someone brushes by me and waves to Harper. She schools her face and gives a polite wave before the mask drops.

Back to anger and rage.

All directed at me.

"Your daughters?" Harper hisses. "What, you couldn't keep it in your pants and knocked some girl up, and that's why you left?"

"Christ, Harper, really? You think I would cheat on you?"

Harper unfurls herself from her chair. I shouldn't be noticing how she looks, but damn. She looks just as good now as the day I met her back in college.

Stunning. Sexy.

She's in a pair of black, skinny pants and a white button-up blouse with puff sleeves. Her long, blonde hair is curled, pulled back with a bejeweled headband—covered in rulers, pencils and apples—that she always loved wearing at school.

Fuck. Harper is really standing in front of me. I always imagined bumping into her, but never thought it would happen.

Now, in the girls' school of all places?

Fuck.

"How the hell would I know, Marcus? You left me, remember?"

"I don't need you to recount our past, Harper." She recoils away from me, like I burned her. "I remember."

"Well, then, you must excuse me because I'm not going to have this conversation with you right now."

Harper stoops over to grab the notebook that fell out of her lap and turns to head into one of the classrooms. Hers, I'm guessing.

Memories I haven't thought about in years slam into

me the second I step foot inside her classroom. Because if there's one thing I remember, it's the way Harper set up her classroom that summer before she started teaching.

I went with her—so I could hang up the things she couldn't reach, she told me.

Pictures from books. Beanbag chairs. Letters. Numbers. Things she made to put on each desk to welcome the students.

So much of our lives back then was wrapped up in my job and playing hockey. Hell, it's what brought the two of us to Nashville to start with. I loved getting to go with her that day and see how excited Harper was for the start of the school year.

But that's not the woman standing in front of me now.

Harper is slipping into a black jacket and throwing a purse over her shoulder.

"That's all you have to say to me?"

Harper ties the trench coat around her and holds on to the ends of the belt. Almost as if she's trying to defend herself against me. It makes my heart ache even thinking about it.

"What do you want me to say? I have nothing left for you, Marcus."

Harper moves to brush by me, but I grab her arm, stopping her in place. "That's it? You're just going to leave?"

"I guess I'm taking a page from your playbook."

Chapter Four

Shoving my key into the lock, I adjust the phone I'm holding between my cheek and shoulder. The ringing echoes before it goes to voicemail.

Shit. I was hoping Angie would answer. Shouldering open my door, I drop my bags on the counter and immediately grab the bottle of wine I picked up on the way home. I wish the parent night was on a Friday. I want to demolish this bottle of wine and not feel terrible, but I can't. Maybe a glass or two since we have school tomorrow.

I'm reeling. In the matter of a few minutes, my entire world shifted on its axis. To run into him at my school of all places? It brings back that sick feeling in my stomach.

Daughters?

I pour myself a larger glass than necessary and take a hearty gulp. The bold taste of the red goes down smooth. Just what I needed tonight.

Kicking off my heels, I drop down onto the couch and prop my feet up.

My apartment is small, but it's perfect for me. It's an older building, meaning I have gorgeous, exposed-brick walls. Hardwood floors are covered in colorful rugs. A small couch faces my TV, sandwiched between two bookshelves filled to the brim with books, knickknacks, and photos.

I moved here after Marcus left. I couldn't stay in the apartment that we had together. The memories were too overwhelming to be there. That whole time was a blur. I was so swept up in my grief that it was hard to function most days.

I was cloaked in bitterness and regret. Held together by tape, tequila, and Oreos. It wasn't until my sister and Angie visited that I was able to pull myself out of my sorrows.

Through tears and a few gallons of paint, we made this place what it is now. The first day of a new Harper—one that was able to stand on her own two feet.

My phone buzzes on the cushion next to me.

Angie. One of my closest friends since college. I dragged her to a hockey pep rally the day I met Marcus. Turns out, she also met her husband, Troy, Marcus's teammate, that same day. The four of us were inseparable. Until *he* left all of us.

"Thank God," I say by way of a hello.

"Hey, babe," Angie's chipper voice answers the phone. "Sorry, I was at dinner with my dads."

"It's Marcus."

"What? What in the world are you talking about?"

"Marcus is the dad to two of the students at my school," I hiss, trying to keep my voice down. I don't know why it matters. I'm sitting alone on my couch in my apartment. It's not like anyone is going to hear me.

"Wait, *Marcus* Marcus?"

I roll my eyes, even though she can't see me. "Yes, *Marcus* Marcus."

"He has kids?" I hear the shock in her voice. "But… how?"

"Angie, come on."

"Sorry. That's not what I mean. I mean, I know how, obviously, but he has kids?"

"Yes."

It's a knife straight to the heart. One that I thought was healed. But one sight of him—one short conversation—and it's cut into pieces again.

Shredded, really.

I guess I never got that closure I thought I had.

"Do you think that's why he left?" Angie asks.

"I mean, why not? I never found out why he left."

I grab the glass of wine sitting on my table and head into the small office. Pulling open the closet door, I pull down the box that I keep tucked away there.

The box that I shouldn't have but can't bring myself to get rid of.

"God, Harper. Are you okay?"

"I don't know," I confess. There's no point in lying. "I don't know what I'm feeling right now."

Yanking off the lid, my lip starts to quiver, my chin shaking as I try to hold off the inevitable tears.

"Do you need me to come visit?"

A tear sneaks out and I wipe it away. "No."

"You sure?"

I pull the pink fabric out and run my fingers over the soft material. I haven't looked at this since I put this dress in the box.

"No. But I don't want you traveling right now when you're so close to popping."

I can feel Angie's smile through the phone. "Hey, I can still travel for a few more weeks. Doctor says the baby and I are doing good. Let me come."

I shake my head. "I'll be okay. I promise."

"Will you?"

"Yes. I made it through the worst days. What's one more?"

"One day at a time, Harper. And if you change your mind, I can have Troy drive me out there."

I laugh. "I love you, Ang. I really do."

"I love you too. I mean it. I'll get my ass out there however I can."

"Love you, babe. Bye."

I hang up the phone and toss it to the side, watching as it bounces off the rug. Gratitude mixed with grief washes through me, knowing I don't have to bear this truth alone.

Pulling out the dress I wore that night, memories flood my mind. Ones I kept trapped tightly inside. I hate that I haven't been able to get rid of these.

But when my sister told me I can't excavate the memories that make me who I am, I kept them.

Under the dress are old photos. Hockey games. Nights in our apartment. Road trips. Silly moments together that I used to think back on and smile.

More tears roll down my face as I pull out the bouquet I carried on our wedding day. A framed photo of us in front of the Vegas sign after we got married. My simple gold wedding band.

That Harper and Marcus were so full of love…of hope for the future.

I want to shout at her. Tell her that within two weeks of that picture being taken, everything would go to shit and she should say no and run away.

Did he cheat on me? Did some woman come into his life and say she was pregnant and that's why he left? We were only together for a year before we got married, but I don't remember him having any other girlfriends.

It's hard not to think about with the date coming up. Our anniversary. Every year, it comes and goes with me in a daze. I used to take the day off school and wallow.

Now? Now, I take the day off to do things that remind me what a badass I am. That I don't need Marcus.

Last year, I met Angie in Cabo for a girls' trip.

The year before that? I went hiking in the Smokies.

Husband? I don't need one.

Taking one last look at the picture and ring, I shove it all back into the box and close the lid on the memories.

I don't know if I've felt that same happiness since then. It's like Marcus took all the happiness I had inside me when he left.

Without a fucking word.

"I hate you, Marcus!" I shout into my closet. "I hate you."

That time, it's with less force as I slump against the wall and let the real tears come. The ones full of anger and sadness at the life that was torn away from me.

All those dreams we talked about that night never came true.

Kids. Trips. Stanley Cup wins.

All of it torn away because Marcus decided he knew best.

I thought I had moved on. I went on dates. I've had boyfriends. Made new friends and memories over the years. It wasn't easy some days, but I did it. I pulled on my big girl pants and did it. If Marcus didn't want me, I'd make my own life on my own.

Until the man came waltzing back into my life when I was least expecting it.

Now what am I going to do?

Welcome
TO
Fabulous
LAS VEGAS
NEVADA

Chapter Five

"You okay, man?" Dax asks, skating up next to me.

"Yeah, I'm good."

"You sure? You're skating like shit today."

Understatement of the century. I feel like shit today. Have for the last few days. After a long day of practice, I can sleep like the dead. These last few days? I haven't been able to sleep a wink.

Last night?

Images of a certain blonde plagued my every thought. It's been five years since I last let myself think of Harper.

Five long years since I last saw that happy face on my feed because of a moment of weakness.

Harper was happy. She had someone wrapped around her that wasn't me and I cracked. Drank too much and was in a stupor for weeks.

And that was because I saw a picture.

The last thing I expected walking into the girls' school last night was running into Harper.

"Thanks for the vote of confidence, Dax."

He throws his hands up in defense. "Hey, you'd call me out if I was skating like shit."

I smirk at him. "As any good captain would. Make sure you're okay."

He butts the end of his stick against my pads. "See? Just making sure you're okay."

"It was a weird night."

"You want to go out and talk about it after practice?"

I shake my head as Coach Andrews blows the whistle. "Nah. I have to get home to the girls."

"They're okay, right?" Dax asks.

"They're good. Giving me a run for my money most days, but they're good."

"Who's giving you a run for your money?" Bode asks, skating over to us and spraying ice over me and Dax.

"You fucker. Really?"

He gives me that cocky smile of his. "Gotta keep you on your toes, Cap."

"Fucking Bode." I shake my head at him as I skate back to the line to resume practice.

It goes by in a blur of missed shots and wide passes. Not a banner day for me by any means. I breathe a sigh of relief when it's finally over.

I always say I earn my keep in practice. It's where you work hard to become the best player, and the games are just a bonus.

Not today.

Today was one of the rougher days.

And all I want to do is go home and collapse.

"WHAT DID OUR TEACHER SAY?" Sadie asks the minute I walk in the door.

"Your teacher?" I ask, wrapping her in a hug before Sam tackles me.

"Yeah." Sadie looks at me like I've lost my mind. "You said if we got good reports we could pick what we make for dinner."

"So did we?" Sam asks.

"Oh, right." I scrub a hand over the back of my head. "Your teacher wasn't there."

"What does that mean?" Sadie asks.

"It means we can still have grilled cheese and apples for dinner. Want to help?"

"Yes!" they both shout at me before running into the kitchen.

"How were they today?" I ask Emma, who is standing behind them.

"Good as always. Sadie read and Sam and I played Uno."

I laugh. "How did that go?"

"I lost epically. I don't know how she gets such good cards all the time."

"She's bad like you!" Sam calls from the kitchen.

"What'd we say about being a gracious winner?" I call back to her.

"It's okay." Emma waves me off. "I'll see you tomorrow, Mr. Evans."

"Thanks."

I shut the door behind her and kick off my shoes into the pile that needs to be straightened by the door. A problem for another day.

All of the ingredients for dinner are spread on the marble countertop by the time I make it in there.

"We're ready!" Both girls are grinning back at me from their stools behind the island.

"Perfect. Want to turn on a show while we make dinner?"

They both nod, and I grab the remote to turn on the living room TV. The open floor plan is nice on the days I need a little distraction.

"Bluey?" they ask in unison.

I groan but turn it on anyway, because I love that little dog. If they knew I actually liked it, they'd likely want to watch something else just to spite me.

The show is background noise as the two of them tell me about their day. These are the moments I love with the girls. As much as they don't get along, they love each other that much more. It's how Jamie and I were growing up. The much cooler older sister and the annoying little brother tagging along.

"It needs more apples," Sam tells me, pushing my hands out of the way and adding more slices to her sandwich.

"Go for it."

The two of them assemble their dinners before washing their hands and heading to their stools to watch the rest of Bluey while I grill the sandwiches.

"Get some carrots out to have with dinner, okay?"

Sadie nods and heads over to the fridge to pull the bag out and drop them onto their waiting plates.

As each sandwich is done, I cut it into fourths for them. "You two eat while I straighten up, okay?"

Sam and Sadie nod at me before pulling their plates toward them and digging in to their sandwiches.

I drop all the dishes into the sink before heading upstairs to start a load of laundry. The sage color paint heading up the stairs is hard to see through all the pictures decorating the walls. School pictures. Zoo trips. Vacations. Pictures of them with their mom and dad. A picture of my dad, their grandpa they won't really remember.

Some days are harder than others, like today where I'm exhausted and could use an extra set of hands. Passing their bathroom and seeing the state it's in, I shut the door to try and ignore the problem. I add that to my mental to-do list. With a practice Saturday afternoon and Sunday off, I should be able to get everything taken care of, if I bribe the girls with watching a movie in the morning.

I could hire someone, but I don't want just anyone coming into our home. I only found Emma through another guy on the team who used her before he got traded.

I'm thankful I have her to help.

Which brings me back to Harper.

Fuck. I try not to think about her, but it's useless. It's like seeing her unlocked the box of memories we had together.

Ignoring the pile of laundry in my room that needs to be done, I head straight into the closet. In the very back is a small box. One I keep tucked away and out of sight. Grabbing it, I sit with my back against the shelves. There's not much in here. A few pictures of the two of us, my wedding ring, and the letter that Harper wrote me when I left for my very first NHL game. It was tucked into my away bag and put the biggest smile on my face when I found it.

I trace my fingers over her pretty handwriting. I always liked to tease her that it was a teacher's handwriting. That it's why she chose the profession she did.

Seeing the words she wrote there makes me question a lot of the choices I made back then. I took the coward's way out. I know that. But it was easier than her leaving me. Because that would have been worse.

The gold metal of my ring is cheap as I rub my thumb against it. The smallest reminder of the love we had.

"Fuck."

This isn't helping anything. The picture of the two of us on our wedding day is one of the last pictures we have together. I couldn't help myself. I wanted Harper more than anything in the world. From the minute I first met her, I was addicted to her.

It's like she was put on this earth just for me. There was no one more perfect. Everything with her was easy from the get-go.

Marrying her on a whim in Vegas? Why not? We were two young kids in love with our futures in front of us.

Maybe that's why things crashed and burned so badly. We'd never had anything test the love we had for one another.

Harper at my games with our kids. A dog. A swing set out back. Everything I envisioned for our family.

All died with a single phone call. We never got it.

Sighing, I place everything back into the small box and tuck it back where I have it stored for safekeeping. I rest my hand on it.

Why haven't I been able to get rid of this?

"Dad?" Sam's voice calls out from the hall.

"Yeah, sweetheart?"

I don't know how much time has passed, but I haven't done a single thing I was supposed to. All because I was distracted by the woman who I couldn't get enough of.

The woman who is no longer mine.

"Can we have dessert?"

"Sure thing."

I can worry about everything else tomorrow.

Chapter Six

HARPER

"Are you sure you don't want me to come with you today?" Rina asks.

"I'm good. I promise." I woke up this morning feeling better.

Grabbing my coat, I lock up my apartment and head out to my car. "I'm a big girl and can go look at houses by myself."

"You don't have to say yes to anything if you don't like it."

I roll my eyes at her even if she can't see me. "I know that."

"Okay. Well, keep me posted on how it goes."

"I will." There's a beat of silence. "Ask."

"Ask what?"

"Rina. You are not as coy as you think you are. You want to know about him."

The first time we had a girls' night together, I had one too many glasses of wine and ended up spilling all about him. And given that she asked at school the next day about any late arrivals, I had to let her know.

She put it together immediately by just his first name. "Can't even say his name, hmm?"

"Rina. Stop it. I can too say his name."

"Then say it," Rina prods. "Just so I know you can."

"Marcus." I spit it out, even though it takes like battery acid on my tongue. "Marcus, Marcus, Marcus."

"You didn't have to say it three times, you know. It's not like Beetlejuice. You're not going to summon him."

"Yeah, but saying it twice is weird."

"Do you want to slap me for making you say it?" Rina laughs.

"Only a little."

Clicking the fob on my car, I drop my bag into the front seat of my small Civic and get in.

"I still love you even when you want to slap me."

"I still love you even when you make me say his name. I'll text you updates."

"Have fun, bye."

"Bye, Rina."

Tossing my phone down, I head toward the first address that my realtor texted me.

I keep thinking about Marcus as I'm driving. I don't know how our paths haven't crossed at school before now, but since his daughters aren't in my class, maybe I won't see him again.

It's okay.

It'll be fine.

Fine.

I wonder how many times I'm going to have to tell myself that to believe it.

I push those thoughts aside for now. I have better things to do today. Like house hunting. It's something I've wanted for so long and it's hard to believe the day is finally here.

Pulling up to the first house—the first in this neighborhood, as there are a few for sale—my realtor is standing outside waiting for me.

"Hey, Harper."

"Hi, Heather."

"Are you excited?" She's brimming with her own as she walks up the short sidewalk to the red brick house in front of us.

"Excited. Nervous. Anxious."

She flips her brown hair over her shoulder and punches a code into the lock box on the door. "Perfectly normal. It's a big life change."

"One I'm ready for."

"Take a look around and let me know if you have any questions."

"Thanks."

The house is different from the pictures. I'm not sure if they made it look better for pictures and then moved things back, but it's different. There's more furniture in here which makes it look that much smaller. The walls are painted a bright purple color.

"This is quite the choice in paint," I tell Heather before walking into the kitchen.

"Definitely something you'd want to change. But the kitchen is fabulous."

"You're not wrong."

It's completely renovated—and stunning. Marble countertops. White subway tile. Light gray cabinets with a darker gray on the bottom. New hardwood floors throughout. Stainless steel appliances.

"Think you could get over a purple living room for this?"

I smile at her. "I think I could manage."

She follows me around the rest of the house as I take in

everything about the small house. The bedroom isn't as nice as the kitchen—it doesn't look like they made many updates to the small room, but I like this place and it's in budget.

"What do you think?" Heather asks when I come back in the living room.

"I like it. Let's see the other one."

"You got it. It's only a few houses down if you want to walk?"

"Sure."

It's a cloudy fall day, but it's an easy walk around the corner.

"I think you'll really love this one," Heather tells me. "It was only just listed last night, which is why I haven't sent it to you. I got in early with the other realtor, so if you like it, we'll have to move fast."

"Does that mean it's good?" I'm excited.

"I'll let you decide." Her smile is bright as we turn the corner and the house comes into view.

"Oh my God. It's gorgeous."

A gray, hardwood house overlooks a small hill behind it with views of the city. The front door is a bright pink that welcomes you inside.

"Just wait until you see the interior." She pushes the door open and lets me go in first.

"Oh my God. Are you kidding?"

The open floor plan flows from the living room through to the kitchen and toward a back deck I can see from the entryway. The living room is focused around a black, stone fireplace.

"I knew you'd love it." Her phone buzzes. "Sorry. I need to take this. I'll be right back."

"Sure, sure." I wave her off as I head into the kitchen to check it out. It's like the other house, but better somehow. I don't know if it's the gold fixtures, the window that overlooks the sweeping backyard, or the fact that the living room walls aren't purple, but it's perfect.

I can imagine walking in here after a long day of work, eating dinner at the island, and then cozying up by the fire with a good book.

It'd be even better with Marcus.

God, I hate myself for even thinking that thought. I don't even know where it came from.

"Sorry about that," Heather tells me, coming back inside.

"No problem."

"My sister is getting married and a wrench got thrown into the plans, so she might have to delay."

"Oh no. What's wrong?"

"Apparently she got married in Vegas a few years back, and they told her they didn't sign some paperwork so the marriage wasn't legal. Turns out, they were wrong."

"What?" That gets my attention.

"It was her college boyfriend. They were drunk off their asses and thought it would be funny, and they were told the paperwork wasn't valid for some reason, but apparently whoever told them that was wrong. So now she's trying to track down this guy to get a divorce before she gets married."

My mouth is suddenly dry. "So she's still married?"

"Yeah. But enough of that. What do you think of the house?"

"The house?"

She looks confused. "Come on. Let's go see the bedrooms."

Right. The house that we're standing in that I'm hoping to buy. Heather leads me through the rest of the house, but I don't see any of it. Refinished hardwood floors in the main bedroom? Don't even notice. Brand-new bathrooms? I can't even look. The dark gray accent wall? Don't care.

What if…what if that's what happened with Marcus and me?

Over the past seven years, I can count on one hand the number of times I thought about him. Okay, fine…maybe two hands. He walked out on me, so why should I give him the time of day?

Except now that I've seen him again, it's hard to push this thought out of my head. Why is this all happening right now?

I'm supposed to be thriving. Buying a house and enjoying a great career. Good friends that I love and a family that I can see when I visit California.

I have a good life.

So why is all of this happening *right now?*

"You think you want to put in an offer?" Heather asks.

"Oh. Yes."

Heather eyes me. "Are you sure? I don't want to force you into anything if you don't want it."

"Can I get back to you tomorrow? Sorry. I'm a little overwhelmed with all of this, and a few days would help to think about everything."

"Absolutely. Why don't you get back to me on Monday? I think we'll be okay."

"And if not?"

She nods, tapping away on her phone. "I'll give you a call, and if you want to get an offer together, we can make it happen."

"Thanks, Heather. I appreciate it."

"We still have a few more places to look at. Want to check them out?"

I shake my head. "Would you mind if we went next

weekend? I love this place and don't think I need to see anything else."

Heather gives me a bright smile. "Sure thing. Keep me posted, okay?"

"Will do."

I watch as she strides down the driveway before I pull out my phone.

My fingers can't type fast enough as I search for the information I'm looking for. The white blank screen as it loads ratchets my panic higher and higher.

I remember that phone call about a week after we got home from Vegas. They asked if we could come back in and sign some paperwork because something was missed and they couldn't file the license. Until we came in, we weren't legally married.

Marcus and I laughed it off. We told ourselves we would do it later. It didn't change how we felt about each other.

We knew we were destined to be married. But to be married this whole time and *not* know it?

This can't be happening.

This really can't be happening.

The website opens and I enter my name.

There in black and white are our names and our marriage date.

We're still married?!

You've got to be kidding me.

WELCOME
TO
Fabulous
LAS VEGA
NEVADA

Chapter Seven

MARCUS

"You looked good out there today, Cap," Coach Andrews tells me. "Better than you did last week."

I take a swig of my water bottle. "My head is back in the game. Sorry, Coach."

"Don't be sorry. I know you have a lot on your plate, so if you need anything, let me know."

"Appreciate it."

"Good." Coach slaps me on the shoulder. "Get a few more laps in out there and then hit the showers."

I nod at him before taking off on the ice. The feel of the ice under my skates helps push everything else from my head. Not a care in the world.

I know my mom has the girls until bedtime. I know they're in good hands, so I don't have to worry.

I push seeing Harper from my mind. That's not going to get me anywhere.

This? Playing hockey? It's what I can focus on. On moving the team forward. We've got a solid team, one that I feel like we can make a deep playoff run with.

Fuck. That's something I never thought would happen.

It always felt like we were the perennial losers of the league. That no one cared about the Knights.

There's an energy in the locker room with these guys for the first time in a long while. I know it has to do with Coach Andrews. I'm glad we have someone like him with the team now. It was a building year when he first came in, and then adding Noah?

Yeah, we've got a team that I'm excited to be a part of.

When all the guys are off the ice, I do a few more laps before heading to the locker room to hit the showers.

Nothing like a good practice to work out whatever I'm feeling off the ice.

"You ready for our game against Vegas?" Dax asks as I pull on a pair of shorts.

"Fuck yeah. We're ready."

"I wish we didn't have to play our first game on the road."

I shrug. "Not the first time we're starting the season in Vegas."

It brings back memories of my very first game. Of everything that happened that night. An impulsive decision to get married to Harper.

I guess some things weren't meant to last.

"I'm ready for the season to start," Dax tells me. "I hate the waiting."

I clap him on the shoulder. "I know. First game will be here before you know it."

Someone pops their head into the locker room. "Yo, Marcus. Someone's at the front office needing to see you."

I drape my towel around my neck and lean back into my locker. "Who is it?"

The security officer shrugs a shoulder. "She wouldn't tell me much. Blonde hair. Blue eyes. Looks like she wants to chop your balls off."

What the fuck?

The only person I can think of that would want to, in his words, chop my balls off, would be Harper. But why the hell would she be here?

"Did she say what she wanted?"

He shakes his head before leaving the locker room.

Never in a million years did I think Harper would be here at the rink. Now? Now I want to see her again.

I never thought I'd get to see her, but now I want to.

One glimpse and I want more. I don't know how I made it through these last seven years without her.

"Who's here to see you?" Noah asks, taking a seat beside me.

"Old flame."

"Old flame?" He raises an eyebrow at me. "I didn't know you had any flames."

"It's Marcus," Graham chimes in from Noah's other side. "He's never shown interest in anyone."

Noah snorts at his remark and I flip both of them off before throwing my towel at them. "Assholes."

"This will be my second full year here, Cap, and I've never heard you mention a woman."

There's a reason for that. I've always been tight-lipped about my personal life. I don't want sympathy from people. They know about the girls, but that's about it. I don't talk about my sister, brother-in-law, or my dad passing away.

And the last thing I'm willing to do is tell them that I walked out on my wife.

Yeah, not a conversation I'm willing to have.

"Sue us if we're curious," Noah agrees. "You're allowed to have a life."

"I'll see you two later." I grab the hoodie in my locker and slide into my sandals before heading toward the front office of the rink.

I shouldn't be excited to see Harper, but I am. Butterflies flutter low in my belly at the thought of seeing her.

I still remember the last time I saw her back then. I was leaving for an away game. She was wearing one of my T-shirts, sitting on the counter of our small kitchen watching as I scarfed down a quick dinner before the flight.

Her hair was piled on top of her head, and her bare legs made it hard to leave. Everything about Harper called to me. She was like a siren, pulling a weary sailor into shore.

I didn't want to leave her.

Knowing now it was the last time I saw her? It still makes my chest raw.

Striding into the lobby, hands in my pockets, I see her. The minute she spots me, Harper's eyes narrow with anger.

What in the world could I have done to piss her off that would warrant her presence here today?

"What are you doing here?" I ask.

"We're still married!" Harper hisses at me.

I rear back, as if she slapped me. *What the fuck?* "What? No we're not."

Harper scoffs, crossing her arms over her black, sleeveless sweater.

"According to the state of Nevada, we are."

I shake my head. "There was an issue with the signatures and we never went back."

It made it a clean break. It's why I walked away from her and turned my back on everything we had.

"Oh no." Harper pokes a finger into my chest. "I was house hunting this weekend and my realtor made some offhand comment about her sister having to get a divorce because she got married in Vegas." I don't miss the way she spits out the word.

"There's no way that's true."

Harper rolls her eyes at me. "Well, I did some digging."

"And?"

"And," Harper starts, fishing something out of her purse, "according to the state of Nevada, we're married."

Harper thrusts a piece of paper into my chest. Opening it, my eyes scan the document. Our marriage license. The one we signed at the small chapel just off the strip.

"They said this wasn't filled out right and we were never married."

The fire in Harper's eyes is enough to scorch me. "I know. I've tried calling and they won't answer. I don't know what is going on, but whatever this is, we need to take care of it."

"Take care of it?"

"Get it annulled." Again with the eye roll. "We're not married, Marcus. We need to take care of this so I can move on with my life."

My eyes scan the document again. "Can we even get it annulled?"

Harper is fuming at me. "Are you saying you want to stay married?"

I shake my head. "But what grounds can we get it annulled on?"

Harper grabs the paper from me and stuffs it back into her purse. "Considering this was filed when we were told it wasn't done correctly is one to start. And if these bone-heads aren't going to call me back, I'm going to go out there and take care of it myself."

I shouldn't be surprised at her solution. If Harper didn't like the one that was presented, she found her own way to solve problems.

Even if it means severing the last tie between the two of us.

Harper is raging and yet, I can't seem to stop staring at her.

Something about the anger coming off her makes her even sexier. Not that I'm going to tell her that, but still.

Damn. I forgot just how beautiful she was.

"I'll go with you."

"What?" That has her looking up at me in shock. "You're not coming with me. I can do this on my own."

"Harper." I step closer to her. I forgot how short she is, even in her heels. "If this is something that we have to take care of, aren't you going to need my signature too?"

"Fuck," she mutters under her breath.

"See?" I use the knuckle of my index finger to tip her chin up so she will look me in the eyes. It's easy to see the way she reacts to my touch. "I have a point."

There's a softness followed immediately by anger. Likely because she felt anything at all.

Harper puts distance between the two of us. "Fine. But I have fall break on Friday and I'm going then. Come if you can; I don't care."

"It's actually perfect because we'll be heading to Vegas for our first game of the season."

"You are?" That has Harper pausing. If I'm guessing, she's remembering my very first game out there.

"Yes. I can meet you there."

Harper taps a finger against her leg. "Fine. You sure the team will be okay with that?"

I nod. "I'll get a few free hours after practice before the game."

Harper nods. "Okay."

"Is your number still the same?"

"Why do you need my number?" Harper asks.

"So I can meet you there?"

Harper mutters something to herself that I can't understand. "Yes, my number is the same."

I rattle the number off to her. It's one of the few that I still have memorized.

"Good. Text me and I'll add yours to my contacts list."

Ouch. That shouldn't sting as much as it does. But why would she keep my number?

"Who's this?" Noah asks, coming up from behind me.

Harper peers over my shoulder before looking back at me. "No one."

She spins on her heel and is out of there.

"You really pissed off no one then," Noah says.

"Who was that?" Graham asks. "And don't say no one, because that was clearly a someone."

I scrub a hand down my face. There's no way I'm getting out of this one. "Want to head to The Sin Bin and grab a drink?"

Graham's face lights up like I gave him an early Christmas gift. I've known the kid since he was a rookie. I think the extent he knows about my life is that I have Sam and Sadie.

All I want is to be the best player I can be and head home to the girls. I want them to have a stable, happy life. They deserve it after everything they've been through. Even if they don't remember anything.

Noah nods. "Sure. Let's go."

WELCOME
TO Fabulous
LAS VEGAS
NEVADA

"Boys. The usual?" Chad, the owner of The Sin Bin, asks as we take our seats in the back of the bar. He drops coasters onto the hardwood table, even though old water rings are etched into the table.

Without any live music at this early hour, the bar is quieter than usual. The voices of happy patrons fill the silence. Neon signs flicker from the wall advertising different beers on tap.

"Please." Noah slides into the booth across from me as Graham takes the empty space next to him. Instinctively, Noah puts an arm around Graham. I don't even know if he knows he is doing it.

My heart pangs and I look away, collecting myself. I remember that comfort. Having someone to be with like that.

Which brings us to the entire reason we're here.

"Ready for the season to start?" Chad asks, setting the drinks down in front of us.

I grab my sparkling water and take a long, refreshing

gulp. "Vegas is a good team, but we've got a solid group of guys."

Chad nods at me. "That's what I like to hear. It's going to be a great season for us."

"Damn straight," Noah agrees.

Chad tips his head in our direction before heading back to the bar.

The wooden, high-backed booths give us privacy, so people coming in and out of the bar don't see us. I like it, considering I don't need any prying ears listening.

"Alright, spill. Who was that?" Noah asks. "And why did she look like she wants to castrate you?"

"She didn't look like she was going to castrate me," I scoff.

Graham eyes me. "Really? That's how I first looked at Noah. And believe you me, I wanted to castrate him some days. Still do, if I'm being honest."

"Hey!" Noah interjects, elbowing Graham in the side. "You love me."

"Not when you beat me at video games."

Noah smirks back at him. "Can't help it if I'm better."

Graham points at the man next to him and eyes me. "See what I have to put up with?"

"See if I let you into the house tonight."

Graham leans back in the booth and takes a long pull of his pale beer and shoots a wink in Noah's direction. "You will."

"As much as I like that idea," Noah starts, "it's not why we're out."

I laugh at the two of them. "Keep going. Don't stop on my account."

Noah turns his attention back to me. "Sorry, Graham likes to be distracting."

"No, I—"

His boyfriend cuts him off with a glare before turning his focus back on me.

"Who was that?"

"Harper. She's my ex."

"Why is your ex-girlfriend coming around the rink?"

It's times like these that I wish I drank. Not that I can't, but I don't like to. I like a clear head for the girls. They deserve the best of me, and alcohol can cloud anyone's judgment. One bad night a few years back taught me that.

"Ex-wife."

The two of them stare at me like I just cracked the code to winning the Stanley Cup. Their faces are exact mirrors of one another—mouths hanging open at the bomb I just dropped.

I've told exactly four people in the world that Harper and I were married. Three of them are no longer here. And the other?

Well, my mom hates Harper, so that is a topic that won't be coming up any time soon.

"Either of you going to say anything?"

"You were married? How did we not know this?" Graham asks, still shocked.

I shake my head and take another sip of my drink. "I don't like talking about it. We did it in Vegas after my first NHL game."

"What happened?" Graham asks.

Noah smacks him on the back of the head. "It's a good thing you're cute because you need to stop interrupting and let Marcus tell us."

"I mean, you're both interrupting me, so really, Graham should smack you on the head too."

Noah throws his hands up in defense immediately. "Hey, I've had concussions. Don't hurt me."

"So that woman?" Graham ignores Noah, turning his attention back to me. "She's your ex-wife?"

I nod. "She was."

"What did she want with you then? Can't say I'd be hanging around my ex," Noah says.

"Apparently we are still married."

"Wait. She is actually your wife? Not your *ex*-wife?" Graham clarifies. "Shit."

"Yeah."

"Why'd you two get divorced?" Noah asks. "Or not divorced, in your case."

I blow out a breath and stare into my drink. This is the part I really don't like talking about.

"I left because my sister and brother-in-law died in a car accident, and a few days later my dad died of a heart attack."

More silence.

Shit. I really do need something stronger than sparkling water as I swallow down the rest of the liquid.

Both of them are staring at me with a mix of pity and sympathy.

"And Sam and Sadie?" Graham asks. "They were your sister's kids? I always assumed they were yours."

"Not many guys are around from back then. Jasper and Bode know, but that's it. And I swore them to secrecy because I don't like the pity. My sister and I always said if anything happened to either one of us, the other would take our kids. I never thought it would happen."

Noah takes a sip of his drink before wiping his mouth and leaning close. "Why did you leave your wife then? Couldn't she have helped?"

"We were twenty-two. She didn't deserve that. Besides, I didn't think we were legally married. But now that turned out to be untrue."

It's a decision that I question on the hard days. When the girls are sick or they are fighting to the point of pulling each other's hair out.

Would this have been easier with Harper?

Did I cut my losses before she inevitably left me?

I don't like thinking about it, but now that she's back, it has me wondering.

"You know you can tell the guys about this, right?" Graham interrupts my wayward thoughts. "They'd want to know."

I shake my head. "The more people that know, the likelier it is to get out. I don't want the girls in the spotlight. I want them to have as normal of a childhood as possible."

"Lots of the guys have kids. Don't you want the help?" Noah asks.

"My mom helps. And I have a nanny that stays with them when I'm traveling. I've basically got it worked out."

Noah slaps Graham on the arm. "How did you not know about this?"

"Ow." He rubs the spot on his arm. "Why are you hitting me? It's not my fault Marcus is a vault."

I smirk at the two of them. They are so obnoxiously in love, it's hard to stomach some days.

"Don't blame him. I doubt I would have told him, even if he would have known to ask."

Noah looks deep in thought as Graham sips his drink.

"Your rookie season," Noah tells me. "You were off for 'personal reasons.' I don't think anyone knew why, but I remember that. Because who takes off two weeks after they start?"

I nod. "The people on the team who needed to know knew. They gave me the time I needed and let me get home to be with the girls after daycare."

It's why when I signed my latest contract I opted for a

no-trade clause. With so much change in their young lives, the last thing I needed was to be uprooted to a new city. Not like I'm going to be traded anytime soon since I'm the captain, but in this game, you never know.

"Damn." Graham whistles. "You know we're here for you, right? I mean, Noah is like an overgrown child most days, but if you need help, we're here."

"I am not." Noah flips him the bird. "I don't know why I love you so much."

I laugh at their antics. "I appreciate it. But don't go telling the others. I don't want anyone to go blabbing about this to the press."

Graham mimes zipping his lips. "Your secret is safe with us. Just know we're here for you."

"Thanks, Flounder."

"Wait. But you said you're not actually divorced. What is actually going on?" Noah asks. "Are you married?"

I waggle my head back and forth. "I have no clue to be honest. According to Harper, we're married. Something her realtor mentioned caused her to do some digging and she figured it out. But now we have to deal with that."

"So you might be married or you might be divorced?" Graham is fighting a smile. "I know you've been through a lot, but man, when you drop a bomb, it explodes."

"And you wonder why I kept it to myself."

"Does Harper know about why you left?" Graham asks.

"She doesn't."

"Damn, Cap. Have you ever thought about telling her?" Noah asks.

"I've never really had the chance before now."

"Do you think you'd feel better if you told her?" Graham asks, flagging Chad down to order another beer.

The sun is sitting lower in the sky and voices chatter on

around us, making it feel claustrophobic. Like airing my personal grief will escape through the relative privacy of the booth into the wrong ears.

Would I feel better? Is that selfish?

"Maybe this is your chance," Noah tells me, pulling me from the fog closing in around me. "Clear the air between the two of you?"

I shrug. I've never thought about it. It seems so far in the past that what good will it do now?

"How'd you meet Harper anyway?" Noah asks when he senses he's not going to get much more from me on that subject.

"College."

I remember it like it was yesterday. She and her best friend, Angie, were at the season kick-off rally and she bounced her way up to me. She looked like an angel with the way her blonde hair shone in the sun.

The minute I met her, I was addicted to her. I wanted Harper and nobody else. Getting married on a whim in Vegas? It made sense for the two of us. I loved her and wanted the entire world to know it.

Except a technicality with the paperwork made it so we supposedly weren't legally married. A technicality that might not be so technical anymore.

I don't know what the hell is going on, but if it means I get to spend time with Harper, then so be it.

Because I haven't been able to stop thinking about her since I ran into the girls' school last week.

Harper. I never imagined seeing her again. She was out of my life for good. I locked her up tight in a box never to think about her because it was too hard. Sure, some days I couldn't help it, but for the most part, my life was good.

I love Sam and Sadie more than anything. They became my world the minute I adopted them, and I have never regretted it. I would do it again in a heartbeat if I had to. I put myself second for them. I've tried dating a few times, but it never stuck.

Maybe it was the universe trying to send me a message. That no one would ever compare to Harper because apparently we've been married this whole time. But based on the way Harper reacted today, the last thing she wants is to stay together.

But what if…

What if this is my second chance with Harper? That nothing has ever happened because I had to figure out my shit before we could be together?

The girls are older now. I'm older. Life has gotten in the way of one of the best things to ever happen to me.

If this really is my second chance with Harper, there is no way in hell I am going to fuck it up.

Vegas was good to us once before. Maybe it'll be good to us again. The start of something new. Something fresh.

Maybe…just, maybe.

Welcome
TO
Fabulous
LAS VEGAS
NEVADA

Chapter Nine

MARCUS

HARPER
What does your schedule look like today?

MARCUS
Practice until 2 then I have to be at the rink by 6 for warm-ups

Meet me at 3 at the chapel

How about I meet you at the hotel so we can talk before we go?

This doesn't require talking, Marcus

Please?

Fine. I'm staying at the Flamingo.
Room 8074

But we're keeping this short and sweet

I'll be there right after practice

Short and sweet, Marcus

I'll text you when I'm on my way

Smiling, I lock my phone and stuff it into the top of my locker before grabbing my stick and heading out to practice. The energy between the guys is a real, live, breathing organism. It's always like this before the first game of the season.

We've played Vegas a few times over the years, but being here now and seeing Harper today? It's bringing back a whole slew of emotions.

I still remember that first assist I ever got, knowing exactly where Harper would be in the stands. Wearing my jersey.

Why is there nothing sexier than a woman wearing your jersey?

"Shooting and passing drills in the neutral zone. After that, we'll break off into three stations. Face-offs, d-point shooting, and one-on-one puck protection." Coach Andrews blows his whistle and everyone skates into action.

This is easy. Something I could do in my sleep. A straight-forward practice before our first game of the season tonight.

Our moves are flowing—everyone is exactly where they need to be as we pass the puck back and forth.

It helps put me in the zone. Being on skates is the one place I can drown out all the noise. It's just me, the ice, and my teammates.

We go through our stations. Everyone is gelling. It feels good. *No.* It feels fucking *great*.

When Coach Andrews blows the whistle, all the guys are grinning from ear to ear.

"Anyone else feel like that was a great practice?" Noah asks. "It wasn't just me."

"I know it's a throwaway, but it did," Graham agrees.

"Glad it wasn't just me," Dax confirms. "Makes me feel good about the season."

"Let's not get ahead of ourselves, boys." Jasper passes by all of us as we head to the visitors' locker room.

I roll my eyes at him. Typical Jasper. He was a pain in the ass my rookie season and has been ever since. More so lately.

"Anyone grabbing a bite before we have to head back?" Bode asks. He changes out of his gear and hangs it in the plain metal stall of the visitors' locker room.

I shake my head as I quickly change and head to the shower. "Nah. I'm good. I'll meet you guys back at the hotel for the ride over."

"Everything okay?" Noah asks.

"I'm good."

Noah studies me. "You sure say that a lot."

I swat at him. "Because it's true."

"Okay."

I don't remember the last time I've ever showered and gotten dressed after practice so fast.

I pull my phone out of my locker and fire off a quick text to Harper.

On my way

"YOU GOT A HOT DATE?" Bode asks, slapping my back as he walks by. "Is that why you're ditching us?"

"Not everything is about women, Bode."

I don't waste any more time as I head out of the arena

and wave to the security guard manning the visitors' entrance.

Hailing a cab, I give him the address and try not to fiddle as I wait through traffic. I'm part nerves, part excitement, wanting to see Harper.

It might very well be the last time ever because she hates me, but after talking to Noah and Graham, I admit she needs to know the truth.

No matter how shitty it is.

The hotel and casino are hopping. A few eyes notice me, but I ignore them, following groups of people to the elevators.

Pushing the button to the eighth floor, I try to gather my thoughts on what I'm going to tell Harper.

Finding her room when I get out of the elevator, I take a deep breath and knock. There's no answer. No sounds from inside.

Did she leave?

Just when I consider knocking again, the door swings open.

There's Harper.

In nothing but a towel wrapped around her torso and her blonde hair dripping down over her shoulders.

"Oh. It's you."

She goes to close the door, but I throw a hand out to stop her. "Why'd you answer the door in a towel?"

"Because I thought you were room service."

Harper slinks inside the room, and the fact that she's not slamming the door in my face is a good sign.

Well, one I interpret as a good sign.

"I know you want to head to the chapel, but would you rather talk now or later?"

"Let me finish changing."

Harper disappears into the bathroom with her clothes before I get an answer out of her.

Shit. This really isn't going well.

Stalking toward the wall of windows that overlooks the strip, I stuff my hands in my pockets. There has to be a way to break this stalemate.

Christ. I scrub a hand over my face and watch the cars and people down below. Signs from the strip are flashing. The sun is blazing hot as it floods the room. Fountains dance on the other side of the street. If we were down there, we'd be jostled by all the people walking with tall drinks in hand.

Pressing a hand to the window, I remember the last time that Harper and I were here.

It seems like a lifetime ago.

Then one call changed everything. The woman in the next room is practically a stranger now. I have no idea what's happened to Harper these last seven years. Where has she lived? Has she been a teacher this entire time? Does she have the same friends?

And God forbid, has she dated?

The thought makes me sick to my stomach.

I have no right to any opinion. I lost it when I walked out. But the thought that Harper could have moved on with someone else doesn't sit well with me.

"You want to talk?"

That sweet voice pulls me out of my spiraling thoughts. I spin on my heel, and the sight of her takes my breath away.

Blonde hair is now dry and flowing over her shoulder. Her lips are shiny, likely from her strawberry shortcake lip balm that she always used. She's in a simple pair of black jeans and a sleeveless denim shirt.

It pulls a smile from my face. She told me it was always

her favorite outfit. That it made her feel like she could take on the world.

I miss that more than anything. Knowing these small things about her that I knew without even trying before. That not many people knew about her.

"You want to sit?"

There's a small couch next to the window. Harper drops down onto the corner of the bed, crossing one leg over the other.

I drop down onto the sofa and scrub my hands over my pant legs. "This isn't easy for me to talk about, Harper, but I need you to know why I left."

My eyes are locked on hers. She sucks in a deep breath, her blue eyes widening. "Okay."

I fist my hands on top of my knees, needing to ground myself. "My sister and brother-in-law died."

"What?" Harper gasps, hand flying to cover her mouth. "Jamie and Dan?"

I nod. "They were driving home late and got into an accident. Sam and Sadie weren't with them, thank God."

"Oh my God. The girls. Your daughters. It's—"

"Sam and Sadie. Jamie and Dan's daughters. I adopted them," I confirm. "They were with my parents that night. I got that call while we were on the road in Seattle."

Understanding dawns on Harper's face, but she doesn't say anything.

"I flew straight home," I continue. "My mom was hysterical. Sobbing. Screaming. I left everything behind and got on a plane. A few days later, my dad died from a sudden heart attack."

"Marcus. Why didn't you tell me?"

I drop my head, squeezing the back of my neck. "My heart got ripped out, Harper. Jamie and I always said we'd take each other's kids if anything happened to the other. It was always said in jest. Something that wouldn't happen. But it did. All of a sudden I had twin one-year-old girls. How was that fair to you?"

Harper's face changes from one of shock to anger. "Fair? Do you want to talk about *fair*, Marcus?"

"Tell me."

"How is it fair that I thought something happened to you? That one morning I woke up and you were there and the next gone? I was terrified, Marcus. Thinking the worst thing happened. The only reason I knew you were okay was because I saw you on TV. I went to the rink that night. Your first game back." Her voice wobbles. "I went to the players' door, wanting to see you. To get answers. Security kicked me out."

I wince. "I'm not proud of that. But I knew if I saw you, I'd cave. You didn't deserve to be tied down."

"I should have been allowed to make that decision, Marcus!" Harper shouts. "You broke my fucking heart by walking out on me. I was a wreck."

Tears slide down Harper's cheeks and they might as well drown me. My heart aches, and my hand shoots up to my chest, rubbing at the familiar feeling. I hate myself for making her cry, for the choices I felt I had to make.

"I know, I—"

"No, you don't!" Harper jumps up, stabbing a finger in my chest as I look up at her. "I had no idea why you left and I was heartbroken. We were married one week, supposedly not the next, and then I was alone the week after. You don't know what that's like. That wasn't fair, Marcus."

Harper is pacing the room now. There's not a lot of space, so I watch her.

"You can hate me if you want," I tell her.

Harper draws up short, resting her hands on her hips.

"That's the problem, Marcus. I don't hate you. It would be so much easier if I did."

"Then what do you feel?" I stand, approaching her with the caution of a lion stalking its prey.

"Sad. I'm heartbroken for you for having to go through all of this alone. For those sweet girls of yours for losing their parents. Your mom for losing her husband, son-in-law, and daughter all in two weeks. I feel sad for me too, because I didn't get to be there for you. I loved Jamie. She was always so nice to me when she came to visit us at school."

A few stray tears escape my eyes. "I'm sorry, Harper. I didn't know how to handle anything back then. I was a twenty-two-year-old idiot who had never had to deal with any hardships in his life."

"I hate how mad at you I am," Harper cries. She bites down hard onto her bottom lip, crossing her arms. "But I'm mad at myself right now too."

"Why?" I whisper.

"Because…" Harper doesn't finish, but instead comes over and wraps me in a hug. I'm shocked senseless, my arms hanging limply at my side. "I'm so mad at you for keeping me in the dark and not telling me. But I'm also so sorry, Marcus. I know how much you loved your sister and Dan. And your dad. I'm so sorry. But mostly I'm mad at myself because I can't be mad at you after you've been through so much."

I hold Harper to me, sinking into the feel of her in my arms. Having Harper in my arms feels like I'm taking the first deep breath in seven years. The calm to the chaos in my life.

I don't know how long we stand like this, but the sweet scent of Harper calms all my frayed nerves. It was always like this.

It won't stay like this. I know it won't. And all too soon, she's pulling back.

Harper wipes the tears from her red-rimmed eyes. "We should get going. I don't want you to be late for the game."

"Right." I clear my throat.

I watch as she shutters her face, closing off her emotions. Backing away from me, she grabs her bag off the bed and is at the door, waiting for me.

"Are you okay?" Harper asks as I follow her out into the hallway.

"I'm good." And for once, it's not a lie. It's like a weight has lifted by sharing this with her. The one person in my world who needed the truth but never got it until now. "I'm sorry to burden you with all of this, but you deserved to know."

Harper nods, clasping her hands around the chain of her purse and walking in front of me. Her mind has to be swimming.

If she needs time and wants to talk to me later, I'll be here.

Because if she wants to talk, that's a good thing.

It might mean an opening to keep talking. And that means we're not out of each other's lives just yet.

WELCOME
TO
Fabulous
LAS VEGAS
NEVADA

Chapter Ten

MARCUS

There's a weirdness in the air between the two of us. Harper has been quiet since I dropped the bomb on her of why I left.

If there's one thing I knew about her, it's that she was always loud and joyful. She was a ray of sunshine from the minute I met her. A southern California girl through and through.

I loved that about her.

It's like her light has dimmed somehow. Under the bright lights of the strip, she's not the brightest star out here.

"Talk to me, Harper."

She's picking at her fingernails. It was always her tell when she was nervous, usually while watching my games. Harper was never nervous around me. That's something that's new.

"It's weird being here now. I never thought I'd come back to Vegas."

"Too many bad memories?"

The light in front of us turns red and we stop. She

looks up at me. Studying me. "We were happy once, right? I didn't make that up?"

I shake my head. "You didn't. We were really happy. I think being here with you was one of the happiest days of my life."

"Mine too." The light changes and the blinking light indicates we can walk. "It's just…messing with my head is all."

"I'm sorry."

The blinking sign of the chapel comes into view. "Let's just get this over with."

"Right."

Get it over with.

Holding the glass door open for Harper, a wall of memories hits me. That happy feeling of walking in here with her on my arm. The anticipation of marrying her.

God, I remember just how much I loved her that day. My very first NHL game. She was there and it was the best damn day of my life, and I wanted to do something big.

Getting married while in Vegas? Why the hell not?

I didn't want to let her get away.

I guess the joke was on me.

"There's a happy couple!" A man with slicked-back, dark hair greets us. A tacky mustache sits above his lip. He's wearing a cheap suit and smells of even cheaper cologne. Or it could be that he's trying to cover up the scent of booze hanging in the air.

She turns to glare at me like I'm the cause of this welcome.

"Don't look at me," I mutter.

"How can I help you? Are you here to get married?"

Harper throws her hair behind her shoulder before plastering on what I can only determine is the world's fakest smile.

"I called this week because we had originally gotten married a few years ago." Harper pulls the same piece of paper she slapped against me onto the glass counter in front of her. "We were told that it wasn't legal because there was a missing signature, but come to find out, it is legal."

The man behind the counter looks stunned for the briefest of seconds before he puts on his happy face again. He picks up the paper she gave him and looks it over. "I'm not sure who told you that, but this is a perfectly legal document."

Harper's smile grows wider and the next words that come out of her mouth are dripping with more fake niceties.

"If it's perfectly legal, then why did we receive a phone call that we had to come back in to sign it in order for our marriage to be valid?"

"Ma'am. I haven't been here long enough to know the specifics. But see here?" The man points to a few different lines. "All valid signatures. You, your husband, and the officiant. I'm sorry you're upset because you got drunk and—"

"We weren't drunk!" Harper yells at the greasy man, slapping her hand on the glass display case. "We were in love!"

Were.

That one word is a knife through the heart.

The man shakes his head, the smile slipping from his face. "Drunk or in love, it's still a valid certificate. I cannot help you. You would need to speak with a lawyer to get it annulled."

"I know that," she snaps. "Why was this information not given to me over the phone?"

"Do you remember who you spoke with?"

She shakes her head. "No, because, as you can imagine, it's quite jarring to be told by someone that works here that the form wasn't filled out correctly only to find out it actually was. And that I'm still married."

The man behind the counter flits his gaze to mine and gives me a quick once-over. "I'm not sure why you're complaining, lady. You're doing better than most people that come in here."

"That's not the point!" Harper screams in frustration.

"Look," I intercede. "We're trying to figure out why we had to come out here to question a marriage license when we were told the signatures weren't valid."

Grabbing the license once again, he gives it another look. "I cannot see why anyone would have called you to tell you this. You and the officiant all signed, so all was in order."

"Could they have gotten us mixed up with another couple?" I ask.

He shrugs. "It's possible. Now, is there anything else you need?"

"Not from you," Harper mumbles.

I try to hide my smile from her. The last thing I want is for her to turn her anger against me. I've already felt enough of that.

"Thank you," I tell the man as Harper grabs the paper and rushes out of the small chapel.

As we turn to leave, there's a couple waiting behind us. They aren't paying us any attention as they hang all over one another and are about two seconds from going at it.

Jesus. I don't think Harper and I were that bad when we were here. We were in love but not nearly as obnoxious.

Harper is waiting for me outside under a bright, flashing light.

Get married in ten minutes by Elvis for $49.99. Includes rings and bouquet! Best deal in Sin City

I wonder how many places say that.

I stuff my hands into my jean pockets as Harper turns on me.

"What a dick," Harper gripes.

"At least we have answers."

Harper swoops her hair up and ties it into a sloppy mess on top of her head. "Answers that are going to cost us."

"I'll take care of it."

"You will?" Adjusting her bag, we both set off toward the main road.

"Yeah. The lawyer fees and whatever costs come with it. I'll handle it."

"I can afford it, you know," Harper tells me.

"I know. But I have the money and maybe my guy will get it done faster."

"Of course you want it done faster."

If it's up to me, I don't want it done at all. But I don't think now is the time to bring that up.

Harper hurries off in front of me as I jog after her to keep up.

"Hey." I grab her elbow and pull her to a stop. People with large drinks pass us as they head toward the action. The sunlight catches on Harper's hair, making her light up like an angel. "I didn't mean it like that."

"Then how'd you mean it?"

Harper looks up at me, wearier than she did earlier. I can't blame her. She had to waste a day off to come out here to deal with this headache. Maybe I should have called to take care of it.

It would've been the easy way out. Getting to spend time with her? I selfishly wanted that.

"You want this over and done with. I'm trying to make it easier on you," I tell her.

"This is all so messed up."

Harper buries her face in her hands. I wish I could pull her into my arms and tell her it's all going to be okay.

It's not my place. She's going to go back to her room, and I'm going to take a cab to the hotel to get ready for the game tonight.

"We'll meet with a lawyer at home and get it figured out, okay? Then you never have to see me again."

She drops her hands from her face, and her blue eyes swim with emotion. "I never wanted this, Marcus."

"Never wanted what?" I take a tentative step closer to her. Off the strip, the sidewalks aren't as busy. Only a few passersby.

"To end up divorced from you."

The pain in her words guts me. I never wanted it either. But I made that decision. I set the events in motion that led us here. Playing the *what-if* game now isn't going to help anyone.

"For what it's worth, I didn't either."

Her lip quivers before she starts walking again. My guess is she wants to hide any emotion she's showing. I give her the space, walking a few paces behind her.

By the time we make it to the crowds of the Strip, I jog up to meet her.

"Let me walk you back to your room?" It comes out as more of a question than anything.

"Sure."

Harper's voice is quiet as we walk side by side in relative silence back to her hotel.

"When do you head home?" I ask.

"Tomorrow morning. Do you guys leave tonight?"

"We're out here for a few more days then head back."

"Who stays with the girls?"

"Their nanny. She's really good with them."

The walk is too short as we stop in front of the lobby entrance. Cars are coming and going as bags are wheeled inside. It's bursting at the seams with people. I spot a few people in Vegas jerseys and move us off to the side.

I know I only have a few more minutes with Harper, but I'm not ready to leave. I can't stall because I have to head to the game. The last thing I need is to be late for the team bus to take us to the rink.

"Look, I know this isn't what you had in mind right now, but thanks for letting me come with you."

Harper nods, giving me a small smile. "I guess I had to, didn't I?"

"You didn't, but I appreciate it."

Harper walks backward toward the bank of elevators. "Good luck tonight."

"Thanks."

I watch her get swallowed up in the crowds before she disappears. Damn. I wish I didn't have to go play for once. I want to follow her up to her room and spend time with her. Talk to her. Make her understand why I did what I did.

We'll have to see each other at home. We'll need to meet to sign papers. Text about it.

My thoughts flow like a reel, catching glimpses of what our life could have been, but it pauses on a scene in the future. One without divorce stamped on the frame. With one last smile, I turn toward my hotel room.

Instead of signing divorce papers…could this be a shot at a second chance with Harper?

Chapter Eleven

I shouldn't be here. I don't even know *why* I'm here.
But I am.

I figure, when in Vegas, why not?

I hold my phone out to the ticket attendant in a yellow vest, and she scans it and waves me in.

A sea of blue swallows me up as fans make their way into the stands beyond the concrete ramps and columns. Pictures of the home team cling to each post as people linger to get drinks, food, and team merch before the game.

I can't remember the last time I was at an NHL game. Maybe a week or so before Marcus left?

I knew I wouldn't be able to sit still in my hotel room all night, so I bought a last-minute ticket to come to the game. I could have done a myriad of other things in Vegas tonight, but this is where I chose to be.

My mind is still reeling from the last few hours. Now that I know the truth about everything that happened, it's hard to wrap my head around. Marcus left because his sister and brother-in-law died, then his dad, and he became dad to their girls.

Hugging my black bomber jacket tighter around me, I step into line with other fans to grab a drink. Everyone around me is excited. It's the first game of the season for them. I feel like the lone stranger here not decked out in the home team's colors.

Ordering my drink, I tap my card on the screen and take the almost overflowing cup and sip on it as I follow the signs to my seat. I'm in the nosebleeds. Shimmying my way through the row, I find my seat and drop down.

I sip on my beer as the seats fill up around me. It's getting closer and closer to the puck dropping, and I can feel the energy in the air.

The excitement. The nerves of whether their team will win.

The people around me are talking about the team. Their favorite players. Who they think is going to win the Cup this year. I love this shared camaraderie between fans.

The lights go off and the noise in the arena rises. Everything about this moment feels familiar. New, but familiar.

It's the same flashing lights on the ice before the teams skate out. The team video to hype up the crowd—showing great plays, goals, and the team jumping on one another in excitement.

When Nashville is announced, boos rain down from every corner. I smile and take a sip of my beer to hide it. Marcus always said they fed off the boos. That it spurred them on to play better to try and beat the home team.

When the home team is announced, it gets louder in here, if that's even possible. As the starting lineup is called out over the loudspeakers, my eyes zero in on number twenty-four.

Marcus.

Even skating with the guys on their end of the ice, he looks good. Marcus always made playing hockey look easy. I know that isn't the truth because I saw the time he put into his training.

Seeing him out here now? I know he'll have only gotten better.

And I'm excited to see him play.

By the time the puck drops, the place is rocking. It doesn't take long for them to settle down because Nashville is putting the puck in the back of the net and lighting the lamp.

Damn. They made that look easy.

It's more of that in the first period before the horn sounds for the first intermission. Nashville is up 2-0.

"We are not looking good out there," one fan near me says.

"Tell me about it. If we didn't trade Roberts, maybe we'd be doing better," the man next to him gripes.

I sip on my beer, listening to them as I take in the banners that hang from the walls. Seeing the years, most of them are old. Seems Vegas hasn't been one of the better teams in the league for a while now.

Interesting. Because when Marcus was drafted, I know Nashville was at the bottom of the league. The worst of the worst.

They're looking good now. When they come out for the second period, the team is fluid. Moving as one, their puck handling skills are strong enough to put another point on the score board.

By the time the game ends, I'm blown away at their talent and skill. They win handily, 5-2.

The excitement from earlier isn't there as fans head

out. I try not to smile at their misery of starting the season 0-1 when my team is 1-0.

My team.

It's been a while since I thought of the Knights like that. Will they still be my team?

I frown, and the fissure in my chest cracks a little wider. Hockey always belonged to Marcus. I loved the sport because I got to watch him play, but it's not mine.

After tonight, I really don't know where the two of us stand. We'll talk when we get back to Nashville. We need to find a lawyer to figure out the logistics of divorce.

Divorce.

It feels like sandpaper. I never thought I'd actually get a divorce from Marcus of all people. When we got married, I thought that was it. That I found my person.

Life was easy then.

Everything feels discombobulated and fuzzy. I don't know what the future is going to bring and I hate that feeling.

That dream house? I lost it because I was so distracted when I found out that I was still married, another couple swooped in and made an offer.

It sucks, but I guess it wasn't the house for me.

Things might need to settle down before I start looking at houses again. Heather should understand. I mean, she's the one that brought up the license issue that made me realize we were still married.

Fuck. Marcus and I are still married. I really don't know how long that is going to take to sink in.

This is not how I pictured spending my fall break. Moving into a new house and decorating? Yes. Trying to untangle the strings of a marriage I thought wasn't actually a marriage to a man I haven't seen in seven years? No.

Like I said, I'll figure it out at home—a house to find, no more hockey, and a husband to divorce.

Chapter Twelve

HARPER

"Harper, how is the school carnival coming along?" Jimmy, our school principal, asks me.

I look at my notes in front of me—a long completed checklist of to-dos for the big festival in two weeks. "We're looking for extra volunteers to help with a few of the activities. Petting zoo, games, dunk tank. If we can get half a dozen or so, I think we'll be ready."

"Great." Jimmy nods. "Let me know if you have any trouble getting people to sign up and I'll start making some calls."

"Thanks."

"And no issues with any of the vendors?"

I shake my head. "No. I've reconfirmed everything with the PTA chair who is working with them and we're on track. It's going to be a great fundraiser this year."

"Good."

I make a few notes about other discussion items before our weekly staff meeting for teachers in lower grades wraps up.

Rina bumps my arm as we walk out of the conference

room. "You know you don't always have to help organize this, right?"

I stuff the pen into the ring of my notebook. "I know, but I like doing it. I have the time, so why not?"

"You could have more of a life if you wanted to." Rina's eyes lock on to something in the lobby.

"What?" My eyes flit to where she's looking and I stop in my tracks.

"I'll see you later," she whispers. *Oh my God!* she mouths.

The minute I landed back in Nashville, Rina was at my door. There were more than a few tears as I told her everything that happened. It's still hard trying to wrap my head around everything Marcus told me. Talking it through with Rina helped, but it still feels so jumbled in my head.

Of course, it didn't help that when I told her everything, she pulled out her phone to search for Marcus. Picture after picture of him playing through the years.

She would not shut up about how gorgeous my husband is.

My husband. That sounds weird to even say. Especially now that I'm seeing him again at school.

There was one thing Rina was not wrong about—how gorgeous Marcus is. Standing in a tight, long-sleeved shirt and jeans, it's unfair how sexy he can look without even trying. His thick, brown hair is disheveled, with a piece flopping over into his brown eyes.

"Hi."

"Marcus. What are you doing here?" I close the distance between the two of us, keeping a foot of space between. A safe amount because from here, I can smell the scent of his cologne. There's a tinge of sweat mixed in, like he just came from hockey practice.

He smirks at me. "Picking up the girls."

"Right. Of course." I mentally slap myself. *Why else would he be here?*

"I was kind of hoping I'd run into you."

"Really?" That has my heart fluttering in my chest. It clearly doesn't know we're not allowed to feel things for Marcus, no matter how much I tell myself that.

He pulls something from behind his back. "Here."

"What's this?"

"Your favorite." Holding out a plastic coffee cup with a shy smile, he says, "It's still the Nutella frap, right? I got it decaf since it's later in the day and you always used to hate drinking caffeine in the afternoon."

I'm stunned into silence.

"Shit. You don't like it."

"No. I still do." I grab the cup from the bottom before he gets any ideas. Our fingers brush as he releases the cup, sending heat rippling through me. I should hate how easily I react to his touch, but something about it is soothing.

Ever since I hugged him in Vegas, my feelings have been chaotic at best when it comes to Marcus.

Do I like him? Hate him? Am mildly annoyed with him?

Needing to steady myself, I sip the drink and let the flavors explode on my tongue. Delicious.

He shrugs a shoulder. "I got the girls something, so I took a shot. Glad you still like it."

I smile back at him. A real, genuine smile because the man still remembers my favorite coffee order. "You know, it's kind of kismet that you're here."

"Why's that?"

Marcus folds his arms across his chest, and I have to do everything in my power not to ogle them. He always had the best biceps. If they weren't covered up with long sleeves, I could see the tattoos there that always drove me crazy.

"What do you need, Harper?"

"What?" My gaze snaps to his, and the smile playing on his lips tells me I'm busted.

Damn it.

"You said it was kismet I was here? Why's that?"

"I need volunteers. Can I go ahead and sign you up?"

"Volunteers? For what?"

"The school's fall carnival. It's next weekend. Think you can swing that?"

Marcus pulls out his phone and taps on a few things. "We have a game Sunday afternoon, so if it's Saturday, I can make it work."

I smile at him. "Good thing it's Saturday then."

Marcus smiles back, his eyes crinkling at the corners with how wide it is. I forgot how much I loved these real smiles of his. It's like he always saved them just for me.

"Just me, or do you need more volunteers?"

"Actually, we could use a few more hands if—"

"Say no more." More tapping on his phone. "I'll get the guys to come help."

"You will?" It can't be that easy, right?

Marcus nods. "I mean, Bode will gripe the entire time, but he'll do it."

"He will? Just like that?"

"I have some pull as the captain of the team."

I smile up at him. "Thanks, I guess. That was easier than I thought."

"If you need anything else, let me know."

"I appreciate it, Marcus."

It's weird saying his name now after it was such a bitter word for me for so long.

"I need to go get the girls," Marcus says, turning and heading toward the library.

"Right. Well, thanks for this." I hold up my cup. "And thanks for helping."

I'm rambling, thanking him so much, but it's because I'm still nervous around him.

He winks at me. "You got it. Text me the details. That is, if you saved my number."

"I might have to scroll through my texts to find it again." I laugh.

More like I never forgot the number, but I don't need to tell him that.

"I'll see you at the carnival then."

"See you then."

I can't wait.

WELCOME
TO Fabulous
LAS VEGAS
NEVADA

Chapter Thirteen

MARCUS

"**O**ur first home game of the season. You ready?" Noah is taping his stick next to me in our locker room.

Bode's rock music is blaring across the room.

It's bright in here. The red carpet—to match the team's colors—is somewhat muted from the overhead lights and years of wear and tear. The Knights logo sits dead center with all of the wooden lockers facing it. There's a small door with a bank of windows that leads to the coach's office and the tunnel that takes us onto the ice.

Being in here is like a home away from home.

I'm flipping the puck that I have saved in my locker from my first ever goal. The rubber is worn down over the years, but before every game, I flip it around. Force of habit.

Hockey players are nothing if not superstitious.

"Fucking finally."

"Are the girls here?" Noah asks.

I shake my head. "Too late for them on a school night. They're watching at home with my mom."

"Do they wear little Evans jerseys?" Noah asks, an obnoxious smile on his face. "Or do they rep their favorite uncle?"

I return his smile. "They actually do wear Fisher jerseys. They love Uncle Flounder."

That wipes the smile off his face and earns me a punch to the bicep. "You're a dick."

Flounder pops his head around Noah. "That's because he knows I'm the favorite."

I point my finger at him. "It better not be because you load them up with sugar they aren't allowed to have."

"He totally does." Noah rats him out. "It's not me."

"Now who's the dick?" Graham gives Noah his own punch to the bicep.

"Ow! That hurt."

"No it didn't. Stop being a baby," Graham goads him.

"It could have if I didn't have such strong biceps."

Graham waggles his eyebrows at his boyfriend and the two of them start whispering back and forth to one another.

I smile as I lean over and drop the puck back into my locker.

"Alright, gentleman." Coach Andrews steps into the center of the locker room, halting all conversation around him. "We've got Boston on the lineup tonight. They're a good team, but I like what I've been seeing from you. We're 3-1 to start the season."

"Fuck yeah, we are!" Bode shouts, hands resting on the butt of his stick.

"I love the energy everyone is bringing to their game. The fans showed up tonight, so let's go out there and give them the best home opener they've ever seen!"

"Hell yeah! Let's go, boys! Knights on three!" Bode

cheers, coming into the center of the locker room. "One, two, three…"

"Knights!" we echo.

I stand at the exit and fist bump every guy on the way out, pumping them up. I meet up with the rest of the starters as we're each called out onto the ice. The noise is electric. Fans along the boards are pounding on the glass as we skate around waiting for the National Anthem to play.

I fucking love the energy before a home game. There's nothing to match it. We're having a good start to the season—nothing I want to jinx—and I'm only hoping we can bring home the W tonight.

We're all ready by the time we're getting into position on the ice. The puck drops and Bode snatches it easily before Boston gets it. He passes it to Jasper who shoots it over to me as I skate into Boston's zone.

Bode is hot on my heels as I watch the pair of guys on D for Boston shout across the ice to set up their own play. But they're no match for us. I shoot the puck back to Bode who dekes out the defense before he sends it flying at the goalie.

He grabs it out of the air and drops it next to him to the defenseman. They take it back up the ice into our zone, but Noah is there waiting for him.

It's more back and forth during the first period when finally Bode and Jasper take off on a breakaway. Fuck, even following behind them, they look impressive. Bode sends the puck flying back to Jasper before it's sneaking between the goalie's legs and lighting the lamp.

The stands explode in noise.

"Fuck yeah!" I skate over to them and jump on top of them. "Great job, Jasper!"

"Let's go, boys!" Jasper taps everyone on the head before we get ready for the puck to drop.

Boston evens up the score before the end of the first period, but we come out of intermission and put an easy two more goals on the scoreboard. They cut the lead to one before the end of the second.

Coach Andrews brings everyone to the bench before the start of the third. "Alright, boys. 3-2. I want you to skate like I know you can and let's close out this game tonight. Bring home the W for our home crowd."

Boston gets the puck to start the third and takes off on a breakaway. Noah is waiting for them and deflects the puck up into the nets. The refs blow the whistle to stop play. The TV screens start flashing between couples as I take a breather.

The kiss cam.

I'm skating around on the ice, keeping my legs warm when I see it.

Wait. That couldn't have been Harper, right? It was just your average blonde-haired woman wearing a hat at a hockey game. I'm only seeing what I want to see.

It's not Harper.

I only wish I was seeing her at a hockey game wearing my jersey.

This time, when the camera pans back, there's no mistaking it.

That's Harper.

I would recognize that face anywhere. A plain black hat sits on top of her head, but she's wearing a red Knights crewneck sweatshirt with our logo splashed across her chest.

Damn, does she ever look sexy.

The giant pair of lips are encouraging her and the man sitting next to her to kiss. Her face is beet red, waving her hands at the guy next to her.

I can see her mouth the words *I don't know him* while the

crowd cheers them on. The man sitting next to her kisses the woman on his other side before the camera cuts away from them, but I can't help the grin that splits my face. Fuck, Harper is adorable.

I can't wait to give her so much shit for this.

"Yo, Evans. Head in the game!" Noah shouts.

I smirk at him before taking my spot for the face-off. Knowing that Harper is here now makes me want to play better.

Back in college, I always wanted to play better for her. Harper brought that out in me.

When the puck comes my way, with Bode skating even with me, we take off. With only one defenseman standing between us and the goalie, I fire the puck over to Bode who dekes him out and sends it back to me, then I'm sending it off the cradle of my stick and it hits the net.

A sea of red explodes around us as Bode skates over to me to congratulate me on my goal. "Hell yeah, baby!"

"Great pass!" I clap Bode on the shoulder as the rest of the guys come over to us.

I smile up into the stands, wishing I knew where Harper was. Wherever she is, I hope she's impressed. I can still picture her back in college when I would score. She'd be the loudest person in the arena, jumping up and down, losing her mind.

That's too much to hope for right now. But the fact that she's here means something. It *has* to mean something.

By the time we put the game away in the third, despite a last-minute attempt by Boston to pull their goalie, we win the game 4-2.

Damn. It's one of the best starts that the Knights have had in a long time. Lots of things seem to be going well lately.

A streak that I'm hoping continues for the team and me personally.

Harper's sudden reappearance in my life has to mean something.

Hopefully a good thing.

WELCOME
TO
Fabulous
LAS VEGAS
NEVADA

Chapter Fourteen

MARCUS

JASPER

Well Sadie loves me the most

Because she can beat you at chess

JASPER

Asswipe

DAX

How come neither loves me the most?

Because you don't babysit them

DAX

That's because Noah and Graham
always do

NOAH

Because they love us the most

They love me the most

GRAHAM

Why are we arguing about this? They
clearly love us all

BODE

I didn't sign up for this

I signed you up

BODE

Kids hate me

JASPER

Are you surprised by this?

DAX

Maybe if you tried to babysit more

I'd trust the girls to babysit Bode, but not
the other way around

BODE

Tell me why I'm supposed to go and
help now?

Because I said so

BODE

Fucker.

Our one day off

You can volunteer for Sam and Sadie's
school for a few hours and then have the
rest of the day off

BODE

Any hot teachers?

New rule

Any time you volunteer at the girls' school,
or any function related to their school, there
will be no hitting on anyone

BODE

You really know how to suck the fun out of
everything

Nashville Prep at 1pm on Saturday

Don't be late

NOAH

Yeah, Bode, don't be late

BODE

Is it too late to ask for a trade?

"**A**re you excited for the carnival today?" I ask Sam, zipping up her coat.

"Kind of."

"Why kind of?"

She shrugs a shoulder. "Jack said there was going to be a petting zoo. The goats scare me."

"You can like the goats. It's okay if you do."

I am one hundred percent the reason they don't like goats, and while I shouldn't be happy about it, I am.

Goats are the fucking worst.

"I do like goats," Sadie confirms as she comes up, zipping her own jacket.

A cold spell has made its way through Nashville this week, making it chillier than normal. I've bundled the girls up in hopes they won't get sick being outside today. The last thing I need is for them to be sick.

"Sadie, maybe you can take Sam to see the goats while I volunteer?" I ask her.

"What will you be doing?" Sam asks.

I shrug. "I don't know, but one of the teachers asked me to volunteer. The guys are coming with me."

That has both girls smiling.

"Uncle Noah will be there?" Sam asks. "Yes! Maybe he can take me to see the goats."

I smile at them. "Who do you think is smellier—Uncle Noah or the goats?"

Sam giggles. "The goats."

"Do you think they're smellier than I am after hockey?"

"You are smelly," Sadie tells me.

"Not as smelly as Uncle Noah, though." I tickle her side.

"Are we able to play all the games too?" Sam asks. "I like the throwing games."

"Can we win prizes?" Sadie asks me.

"Yes, there will be plenty of prizes to win."

"Yes!" Sam pumps a fist. "We'll win them all."

"Make sure you leave some for others," I tell them. They are nothing if not competitive, just like me. "Grab your hats and let's get going."

Both girls grab their sparkly gray hats and shove them on their heads. Haphazard pigtails stick out of each hat.

"I'll win them for both of us," Sadie tells Sam. "That way we can both play with them."

Talk of goats, the carnival, and everything they can win carries us all the way to school. This is one of my favorite parts of being their dad. I've loved watching them come into their personalities and listening to them talk. It won't always be like this, but I'll take it while I can.

While the girls are excited for the carnival, I'm excited for my own reasons.

To see Harper again.

My wife.

Who would have thought that all these years later we'd be in each other's lives again? Harper is so close, but just out of reach. I want her. I didn't get her long enough the first time. Spending the briefest moments with her wasn't enough. I don't know if having her for my entire life would *ever* be enough.

It feels like we might have a second chance. I don't want to jinx it. In fact, I'll do whatever it takes to help force a new connection. If Harper wants me to help at the school carnival, I'll do it. If she wants me in a clown costume, I'll pick out the best one to wear.

I won't say no to anything she asks of me.

By the time we get to the school, it's packed. It takes two laps of the parking lot before I find a spot and get the girls out. Streams of people head toward the big open field behind the school. I find the guys waiting at the main entrance. Sam and Sadie spot them and go running, then get scooped up by Noah and Graham.

"Will you take us to see the goats?" Sam is asking Graham by the time I make it to them.

"Why doesn't your dad take you to see the goats?" he asks her.

I clap him on the shoulder. "That's your job."

"Do you know how many kids are here?" Bode asks. I can't see his eyes behind his sunglasses, but I'm sure they're wide with worry. "I can't handle this."

"Too bad it's too cold for a dunk tank. We could've put you in there no problem."

"Asswipe," he mumbles.

"C'mon, let's go, boys."

Noah and Graham set the girls down and hold their hands as we walk toward the entrance of the carnival.

Two rows of games stretch out behind the check-in booth. The rings of games echo in the field. Sugary sweet smells scent the air. The sounds of animals hit my ears and I groan. I only hope I can stay far, *far* away from them.

"This is unlike any carnival I've ever been to," Noah comments.

"It's the school's biggest fundraiser," I tell him. When we reach the check-in desk, I get tickets for the girls to play games and hand them each a stack.

"How did you get roped into this?"

"It's the girls' school. You volunteer as needed."

"You've never volunteered us before," Graham points out.

A few kids come up and say hi to the girls, distracting me from Graham's question. "Dad, can we go play with them?"

I nod. "Sure. Just make sure you don't go wandering off, okay?"

With so many adults and teachers here, not to mention school security walking the perimeter, I'm not worried about them. Especially with their friends' moms trailing after them.

"Okay!"

"Do you know where we need to check in to volunteer?" I ask the woman sitting at the desk.

If she answers, I don't hear her, because everything else disappears when I see the woman who signed me up walking toward me. "Hi."

"Hi." Harper's voice is sweet. She's wearing a Nashville Prep hoodie with a black vest over it. Jeans cling to her legs, and a black knit cap sits on her head.

She is the most gorgeous woman I've ever met.

"Hi," I repeat, not quite knowing what to say.

"Are you two just going to stand here, or are you going to introduce us?" Bode asks, interrupting us.

The fucker.

"Guys, this is Harper. Harper, meet your volunteers."

She looks around at all of them, giving them a bright smile. "Thanks so much for signing up."

"I—"

I elbow Bode in the side before he can say anything. "Where do you need us, Harper?"

"Follow me."

I'd follow this woman anywhere, but I don't tell her that. The guys trail behind her as Jasper drops back to my side. "That's Harper?"

I nod. "That's Harper."

"Wow."

Harper is handing out assignments when I get up to her.

"Marcus. You're going to be taking tickets at the cotton candy stand."

"Got it. Care to show me where it is?"

Harper points around Jasper. "Up front."

"Nice try," Jasper whispers.

"Damn it," I mutter to myself. I head back the way I came, following my nose to the snack shack. Not only do they have cotton candy, but they're also selling popcorn, nachos, and churros.

"Are you here to take tickets?" a frazzled-looking mom asks me.

"I am."

"Great." She hands over a bucket. "All snacks are one ticket. Think you can manage?"

"I think so."

"Great. They'll let you know if anything is sold out. I need to head over to face painting."

I can't get another word in before she's rushing off and the line starts moving. Taking the tickets is a mindless job. A few times, my eyes spot the girls with their friends. Thankfully, their arms aren't loaded down with prizes they don't need.

Harper? She's nonexistent. No matter how hard my eyes search, I can't find her. So much for getting face time in with her today.

A few people ask for pictures, and I oblige, asking them not to post on social media. I don't want people knowing why I'm here. Considering how long I've been in the league, it's a wonder that I've been able to keep this private as long as I have.

"How are things going over here?" Harper asks, appearing as if out of thin air.

"Good." I take another ticket as I keep the line moving toward the cotton candy booth. Hopping up other people's kids on sugar? Done deal. It means I can also make sure the girls split a cotton candy if they come through.

"I appreciate all the guys helping out."

"No problem. We weren't busy today." I take another ticket, ignoring the curious gaze of the woman I took it from. It's the *I know you, but don't know where from* look that I'm familiar with. "So, did you do anything fun this week?"

"Not really."

"No?" I quirk a brow at her. There's a break in the line, and I cross my arms, staring down at her. "You didn't catch a hockey game by chance?"

"What?" She sounds shocked. "Why would I be at a hockey game?"

"Oh, I don't know." I smile, taking a ticket from a teen who comes through the line. "Might have seen you on the big screen."

"Damn it. How in the world did you catch that when you're supposed to be on the ice?"

I smirk at her. "When there's a break in play, it's easy."

"It seems like you already know what I did." Harper brushes a blonde lock of hair out of her face. "Are you gloating?"

"Not gloating. Just find it interesting you showed up. Didn't feel like kissing the guy next to you?"

"Why would I kiss the random stranger next to me? I don't make a habit of kissing men I don't know."

I step closer to her. "Who do you make a habit of kissing? Your *husband* by chance?"

Watching Harper's reaction, I know she's thinking about it.

"Wouldn't you like to know?"

"I—"

I can't finish before the girls come running up.

"Daddy! Will you come see the goats with us? Noah

took us and they are so fun! We can feed them," Sadie tells me. "They're so cute."

I groan. "I can't, girls. I'm still volunteering here."

Harper crouches low. "Do you want your dad to go see the goats with you?"

"Yes!" they answer together.

Harper glances up at me. "I think I can spare him for a few minutes."

"You'll like these goats, Dad," Sam tells me, grabbing my arm. "They're so cool."

"You don't like goats?" Harper asks, looking confused. "Why don't you like goats?"

"I don't want to talk about it."

The girls giggle next to me, and Sam taps on Harper's shoulder. "He doesn't like goats because one bit his butt."

"Hey, you little rat!" I tickle Sam's side before she and Sadie run off, toward the goats I'm guessing.

The fucking goats.

Harper's sweet laughter fills my ears.

"I'm sorry—one bit your butt?"

"Christ," I groan, scrubbing a hand down my face. "I took the girls to a petting zoo one of their friends had for their birthday, and it chased me around and took a bite out of me."

"Oh my God." Harper doubles over in laughter. "I can only imagine your face when that happened."

"It hurt." I'm indignant. "You try getting chased by goats."

Harper pulls her lips inward, like she's trying to hold in more laughter. "Do you need me to supervise you?"

I nod. "Yes. I need you to make sure none of them try to take a chunk out of me. You wouldn't want them to take out one of Nashville's favorite players, would you?"

"Are you the favorite?" Harper asks, leading the way to the petting zoo.

"Ouch. You're as bad as the girls."

"You make it too easy."

The girls bounce up and down, Noah between them, when the ring of animals comes into view. The look on Noah's face is one of pure giddiness. I'm not sure who is more excited, him or the girls.

"Don't you have somewhere to be?" I prod at Noah.

"Nope." He pops the *p*. "Right where I need to be."

"Noah gave us food for them." Sadie holds up two bags. "He got one for you."

I take the bag from Sadie and resist the urge to flip off my teammate. Wild tufts of fur poke over the fence. One goat is watching me with a particularly evil eye before he sticks his tongue out. With a sigh and a healthy dose of trepidation, I follow my girls to the pen.

The girls tell me to hold out my hand and drop some food on it. I follow their instructions. The goat's tongue is hard against my palm.

"See? They're nice," Sam tells me.

I sigh. The next thing I know, the girls will be asking for a pet goat. "I guess."

Harper taps me on the shoulder. "I need to go check on the other booths."

"Here, finish feeding them." I drop the food into Sam's hand.

"If I don't see you again, thanks for coming today," Harper tells me. "I appreciate it."

"You should know something, Harper." I lean close, whispering in her ear.

"What's that?" I don't miss the small shudder that racks her body, even though I can't see her eyes.

"I will always show up for you."

WELCOME
TO
Fabulous
LAS VEGAS
NEVADA

Chapter Fifteen

MARCUS

"Great practice, boys," I tell the guys as I grab my T-shirt and pull it over my head. "Detroit won't know what hits them tomorrow."

"I'd like to get a few hits in on them," Noah says. After the hit that took him out for the rest of last season, I know Noah would like to get some payback against Detroit.

"Keep it clean," Graham says. "I don't need them coming after you again."

"It's not like it was a targeted hit," Dax points out.

"You're too nice." Bode ruffles his hair as he passes by. Grabbing his leather jacket, he shrugs into it and turns to face all of us. "Alright, we're going out."

"Says who?" I ask, putting on my shoes and socks. "It's a school night."

Bode waves me off like this is a minor inconvenience. Easy for him to say. All he has to worry about is himself.

Well, and maybe not knocking up any of the women he's with.

"Easy. You have a nanny."

"And she's also in school. I can't ask her to stay late all the time."

Bode shrugs. "Your mom?"

I shake my head. "She's not in town. Sorry."

"What about Harper?" Noah asks.

The way Bode's eyes light up, it's like he got an early Christmas gift. "Yes. Get your wife to babysit for you."

"You know she's technically not my wife," I point out.

"According to the state of Nevada, I'm pretty sure she is," Noah says.

"Perfect. Bachelor party."

"You can't have a bachelor party if someone is already married. It would just be a party," Dax points out.

"What, that's it?" Jasper interjects. "You have no other questions for Marcus on why he's still married? Because I have some."

Bode shakes his head. "Nope. He's married. Party."

"We are not having Bode plan anything if we get married," Graham tells Noah. "No way."

"If? Now it's if?" Noah cocks an eyebrow at him.

"Oh shit," I hear Bode whisper.

There's a panicked look on Graham's face. "I…I…"

"Would you put him out of his misery?" Jasper interjects, much to Noah's dismay. "We both know you two are going to get married."

"You couldn't have let him stew a bit longer?" Noah laughs.

"See if I marry you now." Graham flips him the middle finger.

"You love me and you know it." Noah blows him a kiss.

With all of them distracted, I grab my jacket and try to make a break for it but don't make it more than five feet.

"Not so fast, Cap," Bode calls after me. "You're not getting away that easy."

I groan, scrubbing a hand down my face. "Can't you go out without me?"

"Nah. We have to celebrate the fact that you're married."

"I—"

"No exceptions," Bode cuts me off. "You need to live a little. And since you don't have a 'real' wife, you can find someone to go home with."

Every one of the guys groans as we all leave and head out into the parking lot.

"Don't listen to Bode," Jasper tells me. "But he's right that you should probably come out. I think we've seen you once since the season started."

"And that's because you made us volunteer."

I hate that the guys have a point. With the girls having more and more activities after school and on the weekends, every spare minute of time is devoted to them. If I'm not at practice or a game, I'm with them.

Or trying to figure out more ways to see Harper. But I don't tell them that. Even though they already seem to know that I have no life.

"Okay. Let me see if I can get the nanny to stay longer with the girls."

MARCUS

Can you stay later tonight with the girls?

EMMA

Sorry, I can't. I have to study for my
midterm tomorrow

WELL, there goes one person. With my mom in Florida for a few weeks, I really don't have anyone else I can ask. I could call the babysitting service, but the last time they sent someone, the sitter was on their phone the whole time and the girls hated it.

I hate to even ask, but it's worth a shot. Things were good between the two of us at the carnival. Is it too much to hope that she'll say yes?

> I have a massive favor to ask of you

HARPER

What kind of favor?

> A favor to help my girls

Oh yeah?

> The guys—

"DUDE. Tell her it's team bonding," Bode tells me.

"Why are you so close to me?" It's only then that I realize that Bode is reading over my shoulder.

"Because you're going to fuck this up if you tell her we're taking you out. Team bonding will make her want to help you."

I roll my eyes and go back to the partially typed out text.

> The guys need a team bonding night. As their captain, I have to be there

Team bonding, huh?

I wish I didn't have to go, but I need to

"OUCH, MAN."

"Bode, seriously." I shove the man away from me and put some distance between the two of us. "I can handle this."

"Just trying to make sure you don't bail on us. We need to celebrate our groom."

I shake my head, trying not to laugh at how ridiculous he is. The man has never met a night he doesn't want to spend partying.

You're really selling this sob story of not wanting to go

I can think of better things to do than going out with the guys

Maybe this is why they are dragging you out for some team bonding

Probably

What do you say?

What's in it for me?

My unending gratitude?

Nah. I want something else

Like?

I'm not sure…

If it means you'll watch the girls, I'll give you anything you want

Rain check

Really?

Yes. I'll figure out what you can do for me

You're a godsend. The babysitter already picked up the girls

Text me your address. I'll make sure they do their homework and eat a good dinner

Two rain checks

Hmm. I wonder what I can get from you

Anything you want

"ARE YOU IN?" Dax calls out, backing out of the locker room.

"Yeah, I'm in."

I pull up Emma's number and call her to give her an update on the evening. Assuring her she'll get home in time for studying, I end the call and shove my phone in my pocket.

"Fuck yeah. I thought the world would be ending before we could get this guy out." Bode wraps an arm around my shoulders. "Can't party without the Cap."

"Okay. I have one rule."

I stop short, staring at all the guys in front of me. Bode is shaking his head like he expected this, Noah and

Graham are whispering to each other, and Jasper and Dax are leaning against the door to the locker room.

"Of course you do. Let's hear it." Bode braces himself, waggling his fingers for me to continue.

"No one gets arrested."

"Easy." Noah claps his hands together. "Well, maybe not for Bode."

"No one." I look at each man standing in front of me and point a finger at them. "We're not going on a losing streak because one of you decides to do something stupid."

At that, all eyes snap to Bode.

"Hey! I'm offended. I don't do stupid shit," Bode tells us.

"Says who?" Graham fires back.

"Me. I'm careful about who I go home with."

Jasper rolls his eyes. "Does that mean you're not going to pick someone up tonight? Since it's team bonding, as you called it."

"I guess," Bode moans, then laughs, leading us out of the locker room. "Team bonding—maybe next time I'll start with that."

"TO THE MAN OF THE HOUR!" Bode shouts, all of us toasting with shots of tequila.

"Fuck, that burns." I suck on the lime to soothe the sting. "This is why I never go out with you guys."

"If it makes you feel better, we never do shots," Dax tells me.

"That's because you never come out." Bode flags down Chad to order another round.

I don't know how Bode managed, but he got a large

table for all of us in the back of The Sin Bin. I know it's for privacy, but it makes for a nice night not having to worry about anyone else butting in.

"Do I need to have Dax supervise when you guys go out?" I laugh. I sip on the beer I ordered.

With a game tomorrow, I don't want to overdo it. My tolerance is low, always preferring sparkling water over alcohol.

I am making a one-time exception tonight.

"How did I get charged with supervising Bode?" Dax whines.

"Better yet, why am I the only one that has to be supervised?" Bode drinks from his own beer.

"Do you really need us to answer that?" Noah asks. "Really?"

"You're like an eighteen-year-old with a fake ID for the first time," Jasper tells him.

"Seriously, you guys suck." Bode pouts.

"You love us," Jasper says.

"I don't know why."

This is why I love these guys. They're ridiculous most days, but some of the best guys I know. They're good guys, even Bode. Well, maybe deep down for Bode, but I'd do anything for any of them.

Even skipping a night in to hang out with them.

God, I really am old.

"Does anyone want to do—"

"No." Everyone answers Bode without even hearing what he says.

"You don't even know what I was going to suggest."

"Because no one wants to do karaoke with you, Bode," Noah says. "You're a mic hog."

"That's because none of you want to sing."

"Because we don't like karaoke," Jasper says.

"I just need to get you guys out of your bubbles." Bode grins, looking across the table at me. "One time, Cap. I want to hear you sing one time."

I shake my head. "Never gonna happen."

"Fine. Then you have to come to another bar."

"That's the trade-off?" I ask, finishing off my beer. A warm buzz floats through my veins. "I guess I can go to another bar."

"Fuck yeah!" This coming from Dax, as he slaps his hand down on the table. "We never get to hang out like this. I love it."

"Alright, alright. Let's close out and get going."

Because if there is one person that is going to keep these guys in line tonight, it's me. If that means we hit another bar sooner rather than later?

I might be able to head home sooner rather than keep barhopping and get to hang out with Harper for just a few minutes.

I'll take anything I can get with her.

Chapter Sixteen

I don't know why I'm so nervous. When Marcus texted me to come over and stay with the girls, I didn't think twice before saying yes.

It's not like Marcus and I are together for real.

Stepping out of my car, I study the house in front of me. For a professional hockey player, it's not what I imagined he would have. The Cape Cod house is modest. The front porch is small, with hand-painted flowerpots holding pink pansies. The sage green shutters are warm and welcoming.

Of course Marcus has my dream home.

Knocking on the door, the sounds of feet running greet me before a younger woman is answering the door. Two identical faces—blue eyes, with smiles that are missing some teeth, and brown hair—are looking up at me.

"Hi. You must be Harper. I'm Emma," the tallest of the three says. "I appreciate you coming out tonight."

"No problem." I look down at the girls. "Hi. You must be Sam and Sadie."

"I'm Sadie, and that's Sam."

I study the two of them, trying to find any identifiers to distinguish the two. It looks like Sam has a bundle of freckles right below her left eye that Sadie is missing.

Not that I'll need to learn this.

This is a one-off thing. It's not like Marcus will be calling me to watch the girls again.

"C'mon in." Emma waves me in. A staircase is directly in front of me with shiplap walls going up the stairs, painted in the same sage green as the shutters outside. I follow the three of them into the house. It opens into the living room and kitchen. Beyond it, a screened-in porch with open French doors to let in the cool air.

Everything about the kitchen is modern. A sink sits in the middle of the island with black fixtures, and four padded stools face the stove and oven.

Gray walls are covered with pictures of the girls. Bright and happy faces stare up from every surface.

The girls wait by me as Emma hands me a sheet of paper. "I wrote out notes for you, but they're easy. If you need anything, Marcus said you have his number, but I put mine on there just in case."

"Thank you." I glance over it, everything seeming straightforward.

Emma waves goodbye to the girls and then it's the three of us.

"How did you meet our dad?" Sadie asks.

I shrug out of my coat and drape it across one of the seats at the island. It's the question only a kid would ask. "We went to college together."

That's a better answer than *it's complicated*. I don't think I need to get into our dating history.

We dated in college, got married, Marcus left, and now

we're…what? Friends? Friends with feelings? I don't know what we are. That's something to figure out another day.

"You also teach at our school," Sam points out.

"I do. Mrs. Gonzalez is your teacher."

They both nod. "She's really nice."

"She is. She's one of my best friends."

Sam wraps an arm around Sadie's shoulders. "Sadie is my best friend."

"Sam is mine." Sadie returns the hug.

I wish my sister and I were that close. I guess it comes with the territory when you have a twin.

"Well, do you two want to help me make dinner for you?"

"Yes," they both answer.

"We like helping. Daddy lets us make breakfast with him every weekend," Sam tells me. "Can we have spaghetti?"

"Absolutely. Can you show me where it is?" The girls help pull out everything we need, garlic bread included. "What kind of things do you make with your dad?"

"Pancakes and waffles."

I smile at the two of them. They are spitting images of one another, but seeing the two of them now, up close, they have more differences.

"You know." I set the pot down on the stove and flick the gas on. "I've never been very good at making pancakes."

"Really?" they both answer, giggling at the same time.

"Never. I always flip the pancake off the pan and it ends up on the stove."

The two of them exchange furtive whispers. "Maybe Daddy can show you how to make them one morning."

"Maybe."

Before, the thought of spending time with Marcus, any

time at all, would have sent me running in the other direction. Now? Now, I want to spend any time I can with him.

I never thought that would happen

But until I figure out what this thing is between us, I do not need to entertain the idea of coming over in the morning. Or what we could be doing so I could wake up here.

I don't think any of those thoughts at all.

Instead, I turn my attention back to the girls. "Okay. Do you want to help make the sauce?"

"Yes."

Both of them jump down from their seats and start dumping things into the pan I pulled out.

A jar of sauce. A few seasonings. Clearly this isn't the first time they've helped.

Sadie sits on the counter, stirring the sauce as it simmers. Sam drops the pasta into the pot.

"What's your favorite dinner to make?" I ask them.

"My favorite is spaghetti," Sam tells me.

"And I like pancakes," Sadie says.

"That's because you always get chocolate chips." Sam rolls her eyes as I scoot her away from the stove with the water boiling.

"Chocolate chips?" I ask.

"Whoever tells the worst joke gets extra chocolate chips in their pancakes." Sadie continues stirring the sauce before I cover the pan with the lid.

I laugh. "Bad jokes. Okay. What is a good *bad* joke?"

The girls hop down and go to whisper together before Sam asks, "Where does a rose sleep at night?"

I screw my face up in thought. "I don't know. Tell me."

"In a flowerbed," Sadie says.

My laugh might be more exuberant than necessary, but I want these two to like me. "That's a good one."

"Do you have any bad jokes?" Sam asks.

"Knock Knock."

"Who's there?" Sadie replies.

"Orange."

Sam laughs. "We've heard this one."

"Well." I grab the pot of pasta, dump it into the strainer before putting it back in the pot and tossing it with a little olive oil. "I don't have many bad jokes."

"You need to come to pancake breakfast then. We know a lot," Sadie says. "We'll ask Daddy."

It's still weird to hear these two call Marcus *Daddy*.

I always thought when Marcus had kids that it would be with me. The picture of us as a family was so clear to me. Waking up every morning, Marcus with our son or daughter. Us together.

It was all I ever wanted.

Seeing Marcus with the girls at the carnival confirms everything I already knew. He was made to be a father.

I get plates ready for each of us, pour us some milk, and we take our seats at the table. The two of them are chatterboxes all through dinner. It takes us close to an hour to finish.

They tell me all about their favorite things—TV shows, school subjects, friends. You name it, I learn all about it. They ask me the same questions.

Knowing what I know now about these two, they are the happiest little girls in the world. Again, all thanks to their dad.

Glancing at my phone, I see a text from Marcus.

MARCUS

How are they?

HARPER

Great. They helped me with dinner

Did they actually help?

Sometimes they bicker more than they help

They were big helps

Talking my ear off now

That means they like you

That's good

They're good kids

Thanks

Means a lot

I LOCK my phone and set it down, but not before seeing the time.

"I think we need to do the dishes and get ready for bed."

"Okay."

The girls don't argue as they take turns on their stool to rinse off their dishes and put them in the dishwasher.

"Will you show me where your rooms are?"

Taking my hands, they lead me up the stairs. More pictures line this wall. Sam stops halfway up, pointing to a picture.

"That's our real mommy and daddy. They're in heaven."

"Your dad told me."

It's probably one of the few pictures they'll have with their parents. Their mom and dad are sitting in a pumpkin patch, each holding one of the girls. One is crying and the other is more interested in the pumpkin next to them.

"Who is this?" I ask, pointing to the crying baby.

"That's Sadie. Dad says she cried a lot as a baby," Sam tells me.

"You cried too!" Sadie tells her like she knows this.

I look at the picture again as the two of them walk up the stairs, bickering over who cried more. I remember meeting Marcus's sister a few times at school. Jamie was always so kind to me. When she told me she wanted Marcus to propose to me, I almost cried.

By the time I make it upstairs, both girls are waiting in their beds in their shared room. Pink is splashed across the walls. Each twin bed has a canopy surrounding it. Bins of stuffed animals are exploding from one corner of the room. A small table sits in the window with a chess set on top of it.

It's their personalities on display.

"Can you read us a story?" Sam asks.

I drop down onto the foot of her bed and look at both girls. "How about a different kind of story?"

"What kind?" Sadie asks. She's holding a pink stuffed bear that looks like it has seen better days.

"You know, I met your mom."

"You did?" Sam asks.

I nod. "I did. Remember how I told you I knew your dad in college?"

"Did you like our mom?" Sadie asks, a thoughtful look on her face.

"She was so nice to me. Nice like you two." The two of them are eating up every word. "She was really smart too. You know what I remember her doing?"

"What?" they respond in unison.

"She liked to make fun of your dad."

"He can be silly," Sam says.

"Maybe that's why he started bad joke breakfast."

"Did you meet us as babies?" Sadie asks.

"I did. Just a few times, but you were really cute babies."

Sam yawns, snuggling down into her bed. The comforter has butterflies all over it, while Sadie's has rainbows. "I wish we could have a baby brother or sister."

"Me too," Sadie agrees. She follows her twin, snuggling down into bed.

"Well, make sure you tell your dad that." Standing, I tuck both girls in bed and turn on the unicorn nightlight that rests on top of their dresser. "Sleep tight."

"Will you come back, Harper?" Sam asks.

"I hope so."

I don't miss their excitement as I close the door and take my time heading back downstairs. All of the photos show a happy childhood for these two.

It feels like I've missed so much from Marcus's life.

School pictures line the wall. Pictures of the girls with their mom and dad. Marcus playing hockey. Sam and Sadie with his mom. Zoo trips. Beach trips. The walls are filled with nothing but love.

I love that Marcus doesn't try to hide the fact that he's not their biological dad, even though they call him Dad. My favorite picture is at the bottom of the stairs. It's recent, from the looks of it.

All three of them have bright smiles on their faces as they stare at the camera. Standing on the front porch, it looks like it might be the first day of school.

They are happy. That's one of the things I missed most about Marcus. His smile. He always gave it to me so easily. No matter what kind of day I was having, anytime I saw Marcus with the corner of his mouth quirked up, I couldn't help but return it.

I feel my heart clanging around in my chest. I wanted

more of these memories with Marcus. We always talked about having our own family, but instead he created his own.

Without me.

Chapter Seventeen

HARPER

A noise startles me awake. The sound of a car door slamming. The TV is humming in the background. The sound of male voices filters inside, ones that I can hear from my spot on the couch. The clock on the wall ticks close to one in the morning.

Headlights cast long shadows inside the house. Getting up, I peek out the window by the front door. A group of guys are illuminated, Marcus being at the helm.

Smiling to myself, I pull open the front door. "That must have been some team bonding."

"Is this the wife?" one of the guys whispers. "She's hot."

"Fuck off, Bode."

"Please tell me none of you drove." I cross my arms over my chest, glaring at each and every one of them.

"Nah. We got a rideshare," the older man with gray peppering his beard answers. Out of all the men standing on Marcus's front porch, he seems to be the most coherent.

"Don't you have a game tomorrow?" I ask.

"We'll be fine. It's a late game." This from a younger

guy leaning against another man in a loving embrace. I'm not sure which of the two of them is holding the other up.

"Well, I'm glad you had a good time."

"We'll have to remember to call this team bonding for when these two bozos get married." The man indicates to the two who are wrapped around each other.

"Is that not what it was?" I give them my best stern teacher face. It apparently works on drunk men as well as second graders. All of them straighten up. As much as six drunk men can.

"We had to throw a bachelor party."

"This was a bachelor party? Who's getting married?"

"Marcus did."

"More team bonding." Marcus's eyes are glassy. I don't know if he's more drunk or tired.

"What's your name?" I ask the older one in the back.

"Ummm…" he starts.

"You don't know your name?"

"Don't lie to her, Jasper."

"Damn it, Dax. Now she knows my name."

I smile at all of them. "It'd be easy to find all of you on the team's website. You know that, right?"

"You're smart," Dax says.

"Why thank you." I shake my head. "Now, all of you need to go home. I have an early day tomorrow."

"Yes, ma'am." One of the guys salutes me as they all stumble down the stairs back to the awaiting SUV.

"Do you need help?" The last thing I want is for one of these guys to fall and break their ankle and not be able to play. Not that it'd be my fault, but I don't want to take the heat.

"We're good."

They're all laughing by the time the doors of the vehicle slam shut.

"Someone drank too much." I follow Marcus into the living room as he collapses onto his back on the couch.

"You drank too much," Marcus fires back.

There's a smile on his face as he throws an arm over his eyes.

"Is that supposed to be one of your bad jokes?"

"What do you know about bad jokes?"

I drop down onto the coffee table across from Marcus. He flips onto his side to stare at me. Brown eyes meet mine. Even though they're glassy and red-rimmed, it doesn't make the stare any less potent.

"I was told you tell bad jokes over pancakes."

He smiles. The smile that captured my heart back in college.

"The worse, the better."

"I may have even been invited."

Another lazy smile that sends my insides swimming. "Well, if the girls want you there, that means you have to come."

"Oh, really?"

I cross one leg over the other and watch as Marcus's eyes trail the movement.

"Don't make me disappoint them. Disappointing them is the worst feeling in the world."

"Would it disappoint you if I don't come?" I whisper.

"I'd deserve it."

"Why?"

"Because…" Marcus sighs, shutting his eyes.

"Marcus?"

I've lost him. His breathing turns deep. Too many drinks at this late hour and he's passed out.

Grabbing the blanket from the back of the couch, I throw it over Marcus and drink my fill. It's been years since I've gotten to look at him. Really look at him.

He looks the same. Except knowing what he's been through now, I can see the age lines on his face. The faint traces of gray along his temples. It makes him even sexier. And damn it, I can't help what I do next.

I press a kiss to his forehead. "I don't want to disappoint you, Marcus. Not anymore."

Marcus lets out a sigh, his eyes opening the smallest millimeter. "I don't either. It's my biggest regret. A mistake."

"What was a mistake?" I ask.

"Walking away from you seven years ago."

"And now?"

"Now, being with you again? It's the most right thing in the world."

Then he's out.

"Marcus?" I shake his shoulder to no avail. He's snoring.

Shit.

Did he mean that?

Hearing those words, I pray he meant them.

More than anything, my heart wants it to be true.

Maybe this could be our shot at a second chance…

WELCOME
TO Fabulous
LAS VEGAS
NEVADA

Chapter Eighteen

MARCUS

Jesus. Is this going to go on all afternoon? The wipers are working overtime as I slowly navigate my way toward the girls' school. Rain batters my SUV as it comes down in sheets.

The wind is making it hard to stay in my lane. Fucking storms. The last thing I want is to end up in a ditch. It's always the thing I think about when I'm driving in weather like this. It's hard not to when I lost my sister and her husband this way.

Traffic is crawling by the time I make it to the school. Thankfully, there's still plenty of time before I need to be here to pick them up.

The rain pelts me as I dash inside. Another crack of thunder splits the air. Looking at my watch, there's still thirty minutes left before chess club ends. Sadie would never let me pick her up early. Too much practice time lost, she'd tell me. I can't interfere with my burgeoning chess champion.

There are a few parents milling around the lobby, soaking wet like me as we wait for our kids. The library, right off the main office and entrance, is full of different student groups. If I look hard enough, I might be able to see the girls.

A few knowing eyes are staring at me. The last thing I want is to get wrapped up in a conversation about how I'm playing. No matter how well the Knights are doing, fans always have something to say about it. A missed goal? A bad pass? They love thinking they know better than you.

Instead of lingering out here, I head to where I know Harper's classroom is. The thought of seeing her puts a little pep into my step_something that has been missing these last few years.

Everything has been about hockey and the girls. I didn't have time for anything else. I wanted to make sure they had the best life possible after the hand they were dealt at such a young age.

Which meant being the best player I could be. Most days, I'm okay with the decisions I made. Sadie and Sam will always come first.

But now that Harper has crashed back into my life? It's hard not to wonder what would have happened if I hadn't left.

Pushing that thought out of my head, I walk through the art-covered halls of the school and find her classroom. The light shines out of the small window in the door.

She's still here.

"Harper?" I knock on the door and peek my head inside her room. There's no sign of her.

Thunder echoes in the quiet room; there's a bang followed by a hiss.

"Over here." Her hand pops out from under her desk.

I should have known.

Walking over to her, I drop down onto my knees and

see her huddled under her desk. "Still scared of thunderstorms?"

"I'll always be scared of them," she whimpers.

There's not much room, but I fold my body into the tight space next to her. Every inch of my side lines up against Harper.

"You don't have to be scared alone."

Another clap of thunder and Harper grasps my thigh. Her short nails dig into the skin under the hem of my shorts. I should hate how the warmth feels. How her touch can still make me feel things I thought were long dead inside of me.

But I can't.

Because it's Harper.

The only woman I've ever cared about. The only woman I've *ever* loved.

"I'm hoping it blows over soon," she whispers.

Glancing down, I see her eyes are squeezed shut. This isn't the first time I've been with her like this. Harper has hated storms since she and her sister went camping outside and she woke up by herself during one. Apparently her sister didn't want to sleep in the yard, so she went inside without telling Harper.

She's been scared ever since.

One of the endless things I know about the woman sitting next to me. Even after all these years, even after leaving her, I still remember.

Another boom shakes the room. Harper burrows herself into my side. Wrapping an arm around her shoulders, I hold her close. I'm thankful she's not looking at me, because I couldn't hide the smile exploding on my face if I tried.

"It's okay," I whisper. I rub my hand up and down her

arm, trying to get her to stop shaking. "Do you need to tell me your favorite things?"

She laughs, her warm breath seeping through my T-shirt. "I don't know if that will be a good enough distraction."

"It always used to work for you."

Harper tips her head up, resting her chin on my shoulder. Her blue eyes are clouded. Before, I knew exactly what to do to get her through storms. Not something I can do here, crammed under a desk. I could keep her calm through the worst of it.

"Things have changed."

"Tell me anyway."

I don't need the reminder that things have changed between the two of us. One phone call and my entire world blew up all those years ago. I'm living with that reminder every day.

"The beach."

I smile, resting my forehead against hers. I can't help it. I have to be close to her. "You always loved the beach."

"I miss it. Nashville is not close enough to the beach for me."

"Why didn't you move home then? After…you know."

Harper pulls back, her blue eyes wide open.

"I couldn't. I…" Harper licks her lips. "After you left, I needed a fresh start at a new school. By the time I got myself together and made it through that whole school year, I realized I had friends here. A life. Leaving would have been too much for me to take. I'd had enough change, so I stayed."

"I don't need any more change in my life," I agree.

Cupping her cheek, I brush my thumb over the soft skin of her cheek. She doesn't pull away from me. Her teeth are biting her bottom lip.

The storm rages around us, but Harper doesn't seem to notice anymore.

Perfect.

"Did you mean it?" Harper asks.

"Mean what?"

"What you said the other night?"

"Yes."

Harper smiles at me. "Do you even remember what you said?"

I nod. "That leaving you was my biggest regret? I remember."

Resting her hand over my chest, Harper traces the Knights logo there. "It makes me glad I didn't leave."

"Why not?"

Harper looks torn. Like she doesn't know if she should tell me what she's about to say. I don't say a word. Whatever it is, I want to hear it. *Need* to hear it. All I want to hear is how much she wants me to stay.

"Because then you wouldn't be with me right now."

That confession has me pressing my lips to hers.

Holy. Fuck.

Every single nerve of mine lights on fire at the soft touch. It's heaven and hell all at once. Because now that I've had the briefest taste of her, I don't know if I can live without it again.

Before I have the chance to second-guess myself and pull away, she leans into the kiss.

It feels just as right—just as good—as it ever did. It's tender and sweet and it reminds me of everything that was missing in my life.

Her.

Harper.

Harper Smith was the only woman that ever mattered

to me. And with one kiss, every reason why she was the one that mattered most slams into my head.

The way she cared for me. Loved me. Never let my success go to my head. With Harper, everything was easy. Life was good with her.

This kiss has me moving my fingers into her hair to hold her to me. I swallow the soft gasp and swipe my tongue over her bottom lip. She tastes like the strawberry shortcake lip balm she always used to use.

New and familiar all at the same time.

I want to stay here. Relearn everything about Harper that I've missed these last seven years. But the school bell ringing brings me back to reality.

Harper pulls back, but doesn't go far. Her fingers have a tight grip on my wrist that is still cupping her cheek.

Her very *pink* cheeks.

What I wouldn't give to stay here with her for hours. Get lost in her. Learn all the things I've missed these last few years.

But I can't.

"I need to get the girls."

"Right," she whispers. She gives my wrist one last squeeze before scooting out from under the desk and standing. I follow her, staying close.

The rain has slowed to a gentle patter against the window. Harper shuffles the papers on her desk, tucking her hair behind her ear. I don't miss the way she fights the smile playing on her face.

"Looks like the storm passed," I tell her, backing out of the room. I can't get enough of her. My eyes stay locked on her beautiful face.

Harper smiles up at me. "Yeah, I guess it did. All storms do, right?"

"Yeah. I guess they do."

WELCOME
TO
Fabulous
LAS VEGAS
NEVADA

Chapter Nineteen

MARCUS

"You said we could play games, Dad," Sadie tells me.

"I know."

"With no time limit," Sam tacks on. "So we can play as much as we want, right?"

"Right," Sadie agrees.

"As long as you eat your dinner."

I steer the SUV into the parking lot of the local pizza joint and park the car.

"We love pizza, Dad! We'll eat all of it."

"And the salad too." I press the button to turn off the car to the sound of groans.

"I don't like lettuce," Sam tells me.

"You liked lettuce last week," I fire back at her, watching as they unclip themselves from their booster seats.

"Eww. Lettuce is gross. It's slimy."

"Slimy? It's not slimy."

"It was really wet," Sadie chimes in.

"Wet is not slimy."

"It was gross." Sam rolls her eyes at me.

The joys of children.

Opening the door, the two of them hop out and grab my hands as we walk inside. It's a small place, one where people don't pay me any mind when they recognize me. It's one of the draws that keeps us coming here for our weekly pizza night.

The smell of tomato sauce and garlic hits us as we walk inside. Pictures of all kinds of pizza hang on the walls. Arcade games for kids line the back wall, where there's also a window to watch the chefs make the pizzas.

Butcher paper is taped onto each table with a bucket of crayons sitting in the middle.

"There are my favorite customers!"

Sam and Sadie giggle as they head to our usual table in the back near the games.

"Hi Paul!" They greet him in unison.

"How was school today?" he asks them.

Paul, an older man with a brood of at least a dozen grandkids, has always been kind to my girls. With a gray mustache and a bald head, he is never without a smile on his face.

"We started a new book about a girl who solves mysteries with her dog," Sadie tells him, taking her seat across from me.

"I don't know how a dog can solve mysteries," Sam says.

Paul grabs a crayon from the bucket and hands it to her. "Why don't you see if you can figure it out while I make your pizza?"

Sam's brown eyes light up. "Okay! I'll tell you when you come back."

"Attagirl."

Paul gives me a wave before heading back without taking our order. That's the best part of coming here. Paul knows us and will always have our order in at lightning speed.

Paul's Pizzeria is hopping for a Thursday night. The take-out line is snaking around the wall.

"Hi, Miss Smith!"

Harper? Where?

I turn to see where the girls are waving and I spot the woman walking toward us. Nerves burble up in my stomach. I haven't seen Harper since we kissed at the end of last week.

Doesn't mean I haven't been thinking about that kiss ever since.

"Marcus. What are you doing here?"

"It's pizza night!" Sam answers for me. "Daddy takes us out for pizza every week."

"As long as we're good at school," Sadie clarifies.

Harper gets down on her level. "You mean you don't make pizza at home?"

Sadie snaps her gaze to mine. The look there is like I told her Bluey doesn't exist in real life. "Why have we never made pizza before?"

"You like coming to Paul's."

"But why can't we make our own?" Sadie scoffs.

It's not much, but this brief show of attitude makes me nervous for them to become teenagers. All over not making pizza at home.

"Maybe next week for pizza night we can make our own."

Harper's hand is covering her mouth. Those bright blue eyes give her away. They're sparkling with the smile she's hiding.

"What kind of pizza do you get?" Harper asks, once she's composed herself.

"Pepperoni, ham, and olives."

"Olives? You like olives?"

Sadie nods at her as Paul drops off two juice boxes and sparkling water for me. "Olives are my favorite."

"Have you tried olives?" Sam asks her, screwing up her face as she stabs her straw into the hole on her drink.

Harper laughs. "I've tried olives before. Not my favorite."

"Have you had them on pizza?" Sadie asks, pointing a knowing finger at her.

Harper shakes her head. "I don't think I have."

Sam's face lights up. "Dad, can Harper have pizza with us tonight? She has to try it. Please?"

She clasps her hands together under her chin, turning puppy dog eyes on me.

"Why don't you ask Harper and see if she can stay?"

If I ask, I don't know what her answer would be. Would she want to sit here and have pizza with us after that kiss? Would it be too awkward? If the girls ask, she has to say yes. No one can say no to my girls. How I manage to tell them no when I need to is one of life's great mysteries.

"Harper. Will you please have pizza with us?" Sam asks, turning those wide, big eyes on Harper.

"Oh, I don't want to interrupt family pizza night."

I wave her off. "Join us, Harper. Please."

Blue eyes connect with mine. I can see her weighing her decision, probably thinking about our kiss. We haven't been together since then, and seeing her like this brings it all back.

The sweetest of kisses.

It's like it erased the time we weren't together with one moment. Sure, I had my share of women over the years. Situation-ships, if you will. We both knew what we wanted going in. And that was that we didn't want more.

I couldn't bring myself to want more from anyone. Not

when the only woman who mattered is sitting across from me.

Harper.

She's wearing a pair of black leggings, a white T-shirt, and a black jacket. Even in that, she's fucking stunning—all that blonde hair sweeping down in soft waves over her shoulders.

"Okay."

"You can sit next to me." Sadie pats the plastic black booth seat next to her, and Harper drops down next to her.

"Thank you." Harper smiles at Sadie, and the way my daughter looks at her? It's like she hung the moon. "So it's pizza night, huh?"

"Yes." Sadie extends a crayon to her. "And coloring."

"I like coloring," Harper tells her.

"Me too. Can you draw a rainbow?"

Harper nods. "Do you like rainbows?"

This is the one thing I always remembered about Harper. She's a natural at connecting with anyone she meets. It's why Sadie doesn't hesitate in inviting her to sit down next to her. It's one of the many, *many* reasons I fell for her all those years ago.

Sam challenges me in a game of tic-tac-toe while Sadie and Harper draw pictures. I can barely get a word in edgewise since they're chatting her ear off, mainly about school things. It's like they're in their own club because they know everyone.

It's the cutest damn thing how much my girls like her.

Paul brings out the pizza and salad and I divvy it up between the girls. "Remember what I said?" I eye both of them.

Sam rolls her eyes. "We have to eat our salads."

"You don't like salad?" Harper asks, grabbing her own helping.

They both shake their heads, talking over each other. "It's too wet."

"And slimy."

Harper looks at both of them. "Well, salads are one of my favorite foods."

"Really?" Sam asks.

Harper nods. "Yes. So you better eat up before I eat all of yours."

Both girls start gobbling down the leafy greens in front of them.

"How did you do that?" I ask. "That would have taken me all night to do."

She shrugs. "I guess I'm a magician."

"Can you always come over for dinnertime?" I laugh.

Sam looks up, cheeks puffed out before she swallows. "Can Harper come over for dinner every night?"

I smile at her. "Not with those manners, Sam."

"Sam!" Sadie hisses.

"Besides, Harper has her own life. She can't always come over for dinner."

"Maybe for pizza night?" Sadie asks.

Harper takes a slice and bites off the tip. "If I do, does that mean you will try my favorite pizza?"

Both girls nod and Sam asks, "What's your favorite?"

"Hawaiian," I answer for her.

All three of them look at me. "How do you know, Daddy?"

"What if it's changed?" Harper asks, taking another bite of pizza.

There's a slight raise to her eyebrows. Challenging me. I wish it was the two of us sitting here alone. I'd love to ask her if any of her favorite things have changed.

Knowing her, she'd say yes just to piss me off.

Sadie's voice pulls me back into the conversation.

"What's on Hawaiian?" Sadie asks, taking a bite that is too big for her.

"Slow down there," I tell her.

She chews and swallows before waiting on Harper's answer.

"Pineapple and ham."

"Fruit on pizza?" Sam asks. "That sounds weird."

"Do you like our pizza?" Sadie smacks her lips together, a ring of sauce around her mouth.

Harper gives her a smile. "I do. Might be my new favorite."

The girls make quick work of finishing their dinners. Not even the temptation of Harper being at dinner can stop them from wanting to play their games.

"Here." I pull the small stack of quarters from my jacket pocket. "Go play."

"Yes!" they chant together and grab the baggie from my hand and go running toward the games, where they are still in my line of sight.

"For real. Did you like the pizza?" I ask, leaning back in my seat and sipping on my drink.

Harper laughs, shaking her head. "God, no. Who likes olives?"

"My two weirdos." I smile at her. "I remember I always ate yours when they came in your meals."

"You do?" Harper drops her elbows on the table and leans across.

I nod. "I remember everything about my wife."

Harper's eyes widen ever so slightly. "I'm not—"

"You're not what?" I lean across the table. "Because we still haven't met with any lawyers, Harper."

"Only until we can figure out what we're doing next."

"Next?" I cock an eyebrow at her. "I know what I'd like to do next."

"And what's that?"

"I want to kiss you again."

"You do?" she asks, like she can't believe I'm saying it.

"Yes. I've thought about that kiss every day."

"Me too," Harper confesses.

A smile spreads across my face. I couldn't stop it even if I wanted to. And I don't. I want Harper to know exactly how I'm feeling. I don't want to play any games. Something tells me Harper wouldn't appreciate them.

"What does that mean for us?"

"It means—"

"Daddy, look." Sadie comes running back over. "We each got one!"

They're holding up a plastic container with the lids off. Each has a pink ring on their index finger. "I loved these rings when I was little," Harper tells them.

"We got a third for you." Sadie holds out the small yellow container and pops the lid off for her.

"You did?" Harper looks touched as a pink ring of her own spills into her awaiting palm. "Thank you."

She slides it down over her pinky, and it brings back memories of when I slid another ring down her finger.

"We match." Harper wiggles her fingers for the girls to see.

"That was nice of you girls," I tell the twins. "I think it's time to head home. Bath before bed."

"Can Harper come next time?"

"We'll see," I answer them as I drop a few twenties on the table and wave my goodbyes to Paul. When we're outside, I click the fob and let the girls say their goodbyes to Harper before I double-check their seatbelts.

"Hey." I grab Harper's elbow before she can scurry off.

"Yeah?" It doesn't take much to stop her. There's a warmth in her eyes that settles something in me. Some long-lost part of me that I didn't really like to think was missing but actually was.

"Thanks for staying tonight."

Harper looks at the girls through the car window before turning her attention back to me. "You're really good with them."

I squeeze the back of my neck. "Yeah?"

"Yeah. You are their entire world."

I blow out a deep breath. One I didn't even realize I was holding. "I try. I try really hard to give them the best life they can have. Everything I do is for them."

"I know," Harper agrees, squeezing my bicep. "Trust me, I know better than anyone."

There's a million apologies I could give her, but I don't know how far it'll get me with her. She only needs one.

And I'm not quite sure how to word it to her.

"Look, Harper—"

"Take me out."

"Uhh, what?"

There is no possible way I heard her correctly.

"On a date. You remember how those work, right?" There's a smirk playing on her full lips. One I wish I could kiss.

"Funny. I think I can figure out how one works. You want me to take you out?"

"Yes. I think your wife deserves a night out with her husband."

"When?" I fire off. I don't want to give Harper the chance to change her mind.

A date with Harper? I would walk through fire for just one chance to show her I'm not the guy that left her all those years ago.

"When are you home next and don't have a game?"

Fuck. I roll through my schedule in my head. I have it

memorized because I want to make sure I'm always here for the girls. I don't like taking time away from them, but Harper is one of the only people I will sacrifice time with them for.

"Sunday. We have a game tomorrow night and Saturday, then I have Sunday off."

"Are you sure you don't want to spend the day with the girls?" Harper asks.

And this is why I want to make this date happen more than anything. One dinner with them and she is already thinking of them. The same Harper she's always been.

"I'm taking the girls to the zoo, but maybe we can get dinner after?"

Harper nods. "Dinner sounds good."

I step closer, keeping a foot between us. I'm well aware there are two sets of eyes on us. I don't want to let the girls know how much Harper means to me. It's too early for that.

"Perfect. I'll get a babysitter lined up. Dinner."

Harper nods, crossing her arms over her chest. "Perfect."

I can't fight the smile that slides across my face. "Thank you."

Harper backs away, taking a deep breath. Almost like she needs the space from me.

Is she feeling what I'm feeling?

"For what?"

"For giving me a second chance."

Chapter Twenty

HARPER

"Why do I have nothing to wear?"

I'm standing in front of my closet in my robe, with a towel wrapped around my hair, stressing about this date tonight.

"Let me see your options," Angie tells me.

Holding up my phone, I scan the phone over my closet so Angie can see everything I have.

"It's a first date with Marcus," I tell her. "I have to look good."

Angie smiles at me. "You've already had a first date with Marcus, babe."

I roll my eyes dramatically so she can see. "I realize that. You know what I mean."

"Harper, you could show up wearing a unicorn onesie and Marcus would love it because it's you."

I flop backward onto my bed and let the towel fall off my head. "Well, the goal is to maybe have some good sex tonight, so maybe not a unicorn onesie."

Angie gasps. "Finally! You're finally admitting how you feel about Marcus. Thank God!"

"Okay, I'm hanging up on you. This conversation is no longer helpful to me."

"Wait!" Angie stops me. "Wear your black leather leggings with the white bodysuit that dips low—"

"That I can't wear a bra with?"

She smiles back at me, sipping from her water bottle that is the size of my head. Things you need to do when you're pregnant, I guess. "That's the one. Throw in that black blazer of yours, and Marcus will be wanting to pull the car over and have sex before dinner."

"I don't think I'm the only one who will be having sex tonight."

Angie winces. "Please. Troy will not be getting anywhere near me until this baby comes. I feel like a beached whale. If this baby doesn't come before Christmas, I'm going to cry."

"I guarantee Troy does not care, Ang. Go get some from your husband so I don't have to divulge everything Marcus and I do tonight."

She points a finger at me. "As long as you get some."

"Bye, Ang."

"Love you!"

I end the call and dig out the outfit from my closet that I want to wear tonight. I can't believe I didn't think of this. The sheer, lace overlay is the perfect complement for the black faux-leather leggings.

I dry my hair and add some curls to the ends before putting on a little bit of makeup. Nothing excessive, but it helps me feel like my suit of armor is in place.

That no matter what happens tonight, things will be okay.

Because I'm going on a date with Marcus.

I slide on my bodysuit, thankful it has a built-in bra, so

nothing spills out. Putting on my blazer, I fluff my hair and step in front of the mirror.

Perfect.

The bodysuit hints at what's underneath and the leggings? They make my ass look fantastic…if I do say so myself.

I put an extra spritz of perfume on my chest. It's the same perfume I've worn since college. The jasmine scent always used to drive Marcus crazy. I'm hoping for the same effect tonight.

Checking my phone, I'm giddy that Marcus should be here any minute. Stepping into my heels, I throw everything in my purse and drop down onto the couch.

I'm antsy. I don't think I was this nervous on my actual first date with Marcus. In college, I just knew it would work out. I had a bone-deep sense that we would be together forever.

As sure as I knew the sun would come up every morning.

There's so much baggage between the two of us now, that it's hard to separate that out. I know exactly what I want with this man. It might seem fast to anyone on the outside looking in, but is it when you've spent seven years missing this person?

A knock comes at my door, startling me out of my thoughts.

Right on time.

Never one to take my safety for granted, I check the peephole. Marcus is standing there looking as sexy as ever. Rolled-up sleeves expose his sexy forearms. His hands are stuffed into his dark jeans as he waits for me to answer the door.

He looks nervous. Knowing that Marcus is feeling the exact same way as me has me swinging open the door.

The minute he sees me, his jaw drops.

"Fuck. Me." Marcus grabs my hips and steps inside. "Harper. You look—"

"Good?" I tease, draping my arms over his shoulders. Even with my tallest, black heels on, I'm still shorter than Marcus.

"Fucking delicious."

Marcus runs a hand up my side, under my blazer, and drinks his fill of me. His brown eyes are a riot of emotions.

Want. Need. Awe. Excitement.

"You know, we should probably get going so we don't miss our reservation."

"Reservation?" Marcus asks. The lust in his voice has my body humming in anticipation for this night.

"Dinner? The meal you're taking me out to eat." I smile at him. "You need to feed me before you do anything else."

That earns me a smile.

"Still the same old Harper."

I pat the hard muscles of his chest under his black shirt. "C'mon. The sooner we eat, the sooner you can bring me home."

"WOW, MARCUS. THIS PLACE LOOKS GREAT."

The small seafood restaurant is quaint. Wooden tables hold flickering candles. Blue-and-white gingham-cushioned chairs sit at each table. Couples huddle together over shared meals as we bypass all of them for a secluded booth in the back.

"Enjoy your meal."

The host sets down two menus and leaves us be.

Marcus pulls out my chair for me before taking the one next to me.

"I got the recommendation from Jasper. If it's terrible, we can blame him."

I wink at him. "You know I love seafood."

Marcus drops his elbows on the table and leans close. "Still a Cali girl, I see."

I mirror him, getting impossibly close. "You know oysters are still my favorite, right?"

He groans, shutting his eyes. His lashes kiss the top of his cheeks. I remember always being so jealous of his eyelashes.

Why do men always get blessed with the best ones?

"Are you trying to drive me crazy, Harper?"

I adjust my bodysuit, watching as Marcus picks up on the movement. "I don't know. Seems to come pretty naturally to me."

"What am I going to do with you?"

I grab the menu, hiding behind it. "I can think of a few things."

God, I've missed flirting. This fun, back-and-forth with a man who knows exactly what to say to stir up all kinds of things inside of me. No man has ever matched Marcus in that regard.

"Welcome to Southern Hospitality. What can I get you both to drink?" our waiter asks us with a friendly smile in place.

"Sparkling water for me," Marcus tells him.

"Rosé for me."

"And we'll get a plate of the oysters to start."

Marcus sets his menu down and turns his attention back to me. "Can I tell you how beautiful you look tonight?"

"You've already told me that."

"I believe I told you that you look delicious. Not beautiful."

I duck my head below my menu, trying to hide my blush. Being under Marcus's penetrating stare has butterflies threatening to burst out of me.

"Don't hide from me." Marcus pulls the flimsy paper out of my hand. His calloused hand settles over mine on the table.

"It's been a while since I've had any kind of attention like this," I admit. "Not from anyone that mattered anyway."

"Does that mean I matter to you?"

"Yes," I confess. I couldn't hide the truth from him if I wanted. Marcus was always able to read me like an open book. I never shied away from him. I think it's why we connected and fell in love so easily.

"You matter to me too, Harper."

Marcus's thumb is brushing over the top of my hand, making me want to tell him everything he has missed out on over the last seven years. But that's not really first date conversation.

"Can I confess something?" I whisper.

"Always."

"I was nervous about tonight. It's not really a first date, right?"

Marcus shakes his head, hand coming up to cup my cheek. "Hard to have a first date when you're married."

I smile at him. "And when you've had countless other dates together."

"Maybe we can call it a…" Marcus trails off, thinking. "Help me out. What can we call this instead of a first date?"

"A rendezvous?" I answer, but Marcus shakes his head.

"Seems like it's a one-off when you call it that."

"Good to know."

The waiter sets down a tray of oysters and our drinks. "Can I place your dinner orders?"

"I'll have the salmon," I tell him.

"Make it two." Marcus hands over the menus and grabs our drinks. "What shall we toast to?"

"To us."

Marcus smiles. The genuine one that he always saved just for me. The one that came so easily. The one that I loved so much.

"To us," he parrots.

I sip on my rosé, letting the cool bubbles bounce on my tongue. Marcus takes the cocktail fork on the tray of oysters and digs the meat out of the shell.

"Want a bite?" He holds it up to me.

Setting my glass down, I lean over and close my mouth around the tines. Marcus's eyes are wide as a soft moan escapes me.

"So good. Care to try one?" I take the fork from him, but before I can do anything else, Marcus slants his mouth over mine.

The moment his mouth touches mine, I'm sinking into his hold. I'm needy, seeking out his tongue with mine. Fisting my hands into his shirt, I keep him close.

He's controlling the pace. I want more, but he's moving slow. Probably something I should be aware of, given the fact that we're in a restaurant, but I don't seem to care right now.

I want Marcus, and I'll be damned if I don't get him tonight.

"Delicious." Marcus pulls back, licking his lips. Heat is racing through me. I'm ready to pack up our entire dinner and head home after one kiss.

Goose bumps pebble my skin as Marcus and I make

our way through the oysters. The longer we sit here, the antsier I'm getting.

By the time our meals are placed in front of us, I'm rushing to finish.

"You know you can slow down, right?" Marcus says on a laugh, drinking his water.

"I know. But what if I don't want to?"

"Why wouldn't you want to?" Marcus carefully cuts off a bite of his own dish and pops it in his mouth. He chews thoughtfully without saying a word to me. "You doing okay, Harper?"

"You know exactly what you're doing to me, Marcus."

He smiles, cutting off another bite and eating it. "Turnabout is fair play, Harper."

Finishing off my wine, I wipe my mouth and set the napkin down on my empty plate. "I know you'd hate for me to have to call a rideshare home and get started without you."

"That's just mean."

I smirk back at him. "What'd you say? Turnabout is fair play?"

Marcus pulls out his wallet and drops more than enough bills on the table to cover the meal.

"Get your ass in the car, Harper, because I am ready to have my way with you."

I have never moved faster.

Welcome
TO Fabulous
LAS VEGAS
NEVADA

Chapter Twenty-One

MARCUS

Fuck. Me.

I cannot get to Harper's place fast enough. I'm pushing ten over the speed limit—something I never do—but I can't help it. The minute I saw Harper tonight, I wanted to throw our plans out the window.

Dinner? Who needs to eat when they have Harper looking like a dream?

It wasn't just the top she was wearing, hinting at what's underneath. Those damn leather leggings of hers have been driving me wild all night. They cling to her every curve. Curves I want to feel under my hands.

Harper is sitting with her hands under her thighs as I drive us back to her place. I don't know why I chose a place so far away. It seems no matter how close we get, it only gets farther and farther away.

I can't wait that long.

Finding an empty stretch of road—thank God the restaurant was outside the city—I spot a small, deserted clearing and throw the SUV in park.

"What are we doing?" Harper asks, looking confused.

Unbuckling my seatbelt, I turn to face her. "I can't wait a minute longer. Can you?"

Her teeth sink into her plush, bottom lip. Lips I want to feel wrapped around the head of my cock.

"No."

"Good." My smile is cunning. "Get that pretty ass of yours into the backseat."

Harper unbuckles herself and the two of us hop out of the car before climbing into the backseat. I don't let her sit before I'm pulling her onto my lap.

My dick is hard as steel. I roll my hips, letting her feel exactly what she's doing to me.

"Oh my God. Marcus," Harper moans.

"Do you know how ready I am for you?" Fisting my hands in her hair, I tilt her head to the side. "How much I've wanted you all fucking night, Harper?"

"Not as much as I've wanted you."

"How much have you wanted me?" I whisper against her neck. I trail a path of kisses over her throbbing pulse, rubbing my scruff over her smooth skin.

"Since you walked into my apartment tonight."

I pull back. "That long, huh?"

I can just make out her nod through the darkness. Out here, where there's no light pollution from the city, it's hard to see her. My eyes are slowly adjusting. My need for her outweighs the want to have her spread out before me in a bed.

There'll be time for that.

Right now, I need to bury myself inside this woman to calm my raging desire.

Harper leans close, the smell of her perfume overwhelming me. "Get me naked and you'll find out."

I attack her mouth with my own. I swallow each gasp and moan as I ravage her mouth. It's not polite or slow.

It's a giving and taking. What both of us need right now.

Harper's fingers are slowly working the buttons free on my shirt as I shove the blazer off her shoulders.

Her skin feels like pure heaven as I kiss every inch of it. Her hard nipples poke through the thin material of her top.

I trace a finger down the V of her top as it dips low, watching her shudder. I do the same on the other side. It's all I do, repeating the move as she starts to rock over me.

"Touch me, Marcus."

"Where?" I whisper into her skin.

"My breasts. I need to feel your hands on me."

"Aren't they on you?"

Now that my eyes have adjusted, I see the glare Harper aims my direction. "You know what I mean."

Grabbing the strap to her top, I pull it down. Her breast pops free and I'm practically drooling at the sight, the hard nipple begging to be sucked and nibbled.

I flatten my tongue over the tight bud and listen to Harper whimper. My hands roam over her skin as I focus all of my attention on working this woman up. Short nails are digging into my bare shoulders.

There's so much I want to do with Harper, but I know there will be time for that. I will carve out whatever free minutes I have to spend with her.

I pull down the other strap of her bodysuit and lavish that breast with the same attention. Harper's hand moves to my head, clutching me to her. I devour the woman sitting on top of me.

"Marcus. I need you inside of me."

"Are you close?" I press a kiss to her cleavage.

Harper rocks my head back so she can look into my eyes. Even through the darkness, I can make out everything she is feeling. "Yes. I want to come on your dick."

"Take my cock out."

"Condom?" Harper asks as she reaches between us to undo my button and zipper.

I fish my wallet out of my back pocket and hold a foil packet in my hand for her.

Her hands are warm and small over my long length, but I'm thrusting into her hold. Harper makes quick work of sheathing my dick.

"Turn around. Hold on to the seat."

I wiggle her leggings down her thighs and pull her back on top of me. I unsnap the clasps to her bodysuit and find her bare.

"You've been like this all night for me?" I push a finger inside of her.

"Yes. I want you so badly, Marcus."

Hearing Harper beg has me pulling my finger out and lining my cock up with her pussy. There's no point in waiting. Not when she wants me as badly as I want her.

I push slowly inside, eyes rolling in my head at how fucking good it feels.

"Fuck, yes," I bite out.

"Mmm." Harper is purring in my arms by the time I'm all the way inside her.

"You feel amazing." I kiss each notch in her back as I let her adjust to my size. My hands play with her breasts, tweaking them as she arches into my touch.

"Fuck me, Marcus. Oh God, fuck me."

I brush her long locks to the side and tug her back closer to me so I can nibble on her ear lobe. "Whatever you want, Harper."

I'm not slow. My hips set a punishing pace as Harper holds on to the back of the front seat.

Every thrust into her lights each nerve inside of me on fire.

"Marcus! Holy shit!" Harper isn't quiet. With each piston of my hips inside her, her walls are squeezing my dick.

"C'mon, baby. I need to feel you come."

"Make me come then," Harper fires back.

I reach around her to find her clit and strum my fingers over it. Based on the way she's choking my cock, she loves it.

"I can't wait to feel you come all over me."

"I'm right there."

"C'mon, Harper." I lick and suck on her shoulder. "I know my wife wants to come for me. Come like the good little girl that she is."

"Marcus!" Harper shouts. "Oh my God!"

She's detonating around me. "Fuck, yes."

Holding onto the back of the seat, I keep jacking my hips up into her. Every pulse and flutter has my balls drawing up tight until I can't hold back any longer.

"Fuck!" My moves are uncoordinated as I pour my release into the condom. "Holy shit. Holy shit, Harper."

I nearly black out from coming so hard. I slow my hips down as Harper leans back into me. She's a noodle in my arms as I hold her to my chest. I press kisses into her neck and shoulder, as her breathing slowly starts to even out.

"Marcus. That was—"

"Incredible?"

"Yeah, you could say that."

Pulling out, I tie off the condom and drop it on the floor, making a note to take care of it later. I adjust Harper in my arms, cradling her to me. My fingers comb through the soft locks of her now messy hair.

Her skin is warm against mine. Our breaths mingle in the cool air inside the car.

"Well, there's a lot more where that came from."

Because I don't ever plan to stop doing this with Harper.

Not now. Not ever.

WELCOME
TO
Fabulous
LAS VEGAS
NEVADA

Chapter Twenty-Two

MARCUS

"You want to go out with us tonight, Cap?" Bode asks, dropping down into the seat in front of me. After a win in Phoenix tonight, we're spending the night before heading to Salt Lake tomorrow. One more road game then we're heading home.

Fucking finally. I hate long road trips. Always have. I never like being away from the girls. I feel bad having to have others stay with them.

And now? Now I don't like being away from Harper.

Having had to leave only two days after our date, I didn't get enough. One night together will *never* be enough.

"I'm not really feeling up to going out."

The win tonight was hard fought. Phoenix battled with us to the very end. Only when Dax caught a breakaway at the end of the third period were we able to seal the victory.

"A win like that deserves to be celebrated."

I shake my head. "No way, Bode. I'm wiped. I want to go to my room, see how the girls are doing, and crash."

He rolls his eyes at me. "Okay, how about instead of

going out, we play some video games and call it a night? Is that better?"

"I'm game," Dax says, dropping into the seat next to me. "Too much adrenaline to go to bed."

"Hell yeah!" Bode holds out his fist for a bump. "That was a fucking awesome goal."

"C'mon, Marcus. It's not like Bode is going to let up easily."

"I guess so. But we're going to your room. When I want to leave, I want to leave."

Bode throws his hands up. "You got it."

Noah, Graham, and Jasper get on the bus and take the seats opposite us. "Video games in Bode's room," I tell them.

Graham looks confused. "Why is Cap inviting us to play video games? Anyone else think that's weird?"

I flip him the bird. "We're playing video games because I don't want to go out and this is the only way to keep Bode off my ass."

Graham and Noah both nod. "That makes more sense," Noah tells me. "I'm always game. Especially if it means kicking your ass."

"Har, har," I deadpan.

The bus pulls out of the parking lot at the rink and heads to our hotel. The guys are all chirping who is going to beat who as I pull my phone from my pocket.

HARPER

Hey. You guys looked good out there tonight

MARCUS

Did we?

Stop it. You know you looked good

I know. But I like hearing you say it

What else do you like hearing me say 😉

I can think of one or two things

Are you alone?

No <<surrounded by idiots gif>>

Poor baby

Please feel bad for me

I have to keep these guys in line

Too bad. I was hoping you could call

FUCK. Now I'm wondering if I can get out of this. But Bode calls my bluff the minute we're back at the hotel.

"You can't back out now. We need you for even pairs to match up."

"You only have two controllers," I point out.

"Round robin style. Each group plays another and then the victor from each will play each other."

"You realize you're missing one group, right?" Jasper tells him.

"Nah. I think you and Cap need to battle it out to see who will play the other team. That's only fair."

Pressing the up button for the elevator, I give Bode a look. "How is that fair?"

"You're the Captain. You have an unfair advantage."

"In video games?" When the doors open, I step inside and press the button to the fifth floor. "How do I have an advantage?"

"Dunno, you just do."

Bode ends his argument in a way only he can. I shake my head at him when the elevator dings on my floor. "I'm going to change and check on the girls. Meet up with you in a few."

"No backing out!" is the last thing that's shouted at me as the doors close. One of the perks of being the captain is I get my own room on the road.

Thank fuck.

Because the last thing I want to do is chat with one of the guys. Not that I don't love my team, but after a win like tonight's, I need silence in order to decompress.

MARCUS

How were the girls tonight?

EMMA

Good, as usual

Spent most of the night working on their books they're writing for school

Were they able to get them done?

Done, colored, and ready to read to the class

Thanks. Appreciate it

I SMILE to myself as I loosen the knot in my tie when I enter my room. The girls had picture books to write and illustrate for their upcoming project. It was all about puppies, chess, and hockey.

A weird combination if you ask me, but puppies playing hockey and chess?

I'd read it.

Changing into a pair of athletic shorts and a red Knights hoodie, I slide into my tennis shoes and head back upstairs.

MARCUS

I wish I could call you instead of hanging with the guys

HARPER

You'll be home soon enough

In three days

Feels like forever

Feels like it since I last saw you

It's been a week

A week too long

IT'S amazing how easily she's slotted herself back into my life. When we're not together, we're always texting.

I can't wait to see you

Me too

I've got the girls Friday night, but want to do dinner and hang out after bed?

Hanging out? Is that what the kids are calling it these days?

> If it gets you to come over, we can call it whatever you want

> I'll see you then

LOCKING MY PHONE, I knock on Bode's door. I can already hear shouts before Jasper pulls open the door. "Thanks for showing up. I won twenty bucks from Bode."

I laugh, closing the door behind me. "Glad I could help you win."

"I thought for sure you'd bail," Bode tells me, slapping a twenty into Jasper's palm.

"The chance to kick Bode's ass in video games? I'll always show up for that."

Bode snorts. "Whatever you say."

"At least you're not getting me drunk this time."

"You could barely hang last time," Dax points out, as he is drinking from a bottle of water.

"Is this you trying to hang?" I push his legs out of the way and drop down onto the bed.

Noah and Graham are currently battling it out, their little characters driving all over the road. They're yelling at one another, elbowing each other's sides to try and win.

I laugh and take out my buzzing phone, hoping it's Harper.

MOM

> Great game tonight

> You skated hard

> I'm excited to see you and the girls soon

MARCUS

We're excited to see you too

They're really excited to show you their new books they made

I heard all about it when Emma called me tonight

Let me know if you need me to pick you up from the airport

Sheila is driving us home, but thanks, son

Sounds good. Enjoy the rest of your trip

SOMETHING STIRS DEEP in my gut. The one thing I'm not looking forward to? Telling her about Harper. That's something that I'll need to figure out. Because she has not liked her for a long time.

Seven years to be exact.

But right now, I push that to the side and take the controller that Noah tosses my way as he concedes his loss to Graham.

I have a feeling neither of them will really be losing based on the look they share.

"You ready to lose?" Bode asks me as he fires up another game.

I burst out laughing. "Oh, Bode. I needed that laugh."

"You're a dick. Prepare to have your ass kicked."

"Damn. I don't know if I've ever seen you like this," Jasper says from his spot on the chair.

"Like what?" I don't look at him, but can imagine what his face looks like. He might be the one person who is grumpier than me.

"I don't know—happy."

I smile at him, giving him a quick side-eye so I don't lose focus. "Something about beating Bode brings me so much joy."

"Damn. See if I invite you guys over to play video games again."

"You know," Noah starts, "it means Bode loves us because he's skipping a night out with a girl."

"I'm beginning to question why."

Bode easily overtakes me with his character but then I take it right back. The two of us go back and forth until he edges me out at the last minute.

Jasper laughs before he takes his spot to play. He's stuffing his phone into his pocket. "Who are you talking to?"

"Why am I talking to anyone?" he asks.

"Because you were laughing at your phone," Dax agrees. "You two are happy tonight. It's weird."

"Anyone else think Dax is starting to sound like Bode?" I ask.

"Hey! I do not." Dax looks affronted. "Do I?"

"Not a bad thing, Dax," Bode tells him.

"Great, now I know it's a bad thing," Dax whines.

"I want to go back to this whole Jasper and Marcus being happy." Noah diverts the conversation back to me and Jasper, causing us both to groan.

"Why are you so interested?" I take Jasper's seat in the chair by the window and kick my feet up onto the table.

"Are you and Harper an item now?" Graham asks me. "Is that why you're so happy?"

The game pauses, quieting all noise in the room. Shit. This was not something I wanted to discuss with the guys right now.

Things are still new with Harper. Do I want them to be

more? Yes. But I don't want to jinx anything. Call it my superstition. I had *hoped* to keep things between the two of us, but based on all the faces looking at me, I won't be able to keep them at bay.

"It's still new."

"That means there is a thing." Noah waggles his eyebrows at me.

"Jesus. You've all been spending way too much time together."

Jasper gives me a knowing smile and I send the attention right back to him. "What about Jasper? He's looking pretty smug over there."

"Dick move, Cap. Dick move." He flips me off.

"You've been smiling more too. It's weird," Bode comments.

"You know we can smile, right?" I ask him. "Mouths are made to smile."

"Not yours," Bode says. "Either of yours."

"If I have to tell, so do you," I tell Jasper.

"I want it on record I hate you all." Jasper rolls his eyes at us. "I signed up for a dating app."

I don't know if it's possible, but the room has gotten even quieter. It takes a lot to get this group of guys to shut up.

"You signed up for a dating app?" Bode is appalled. "Dude. You're a hockey player. You know how easy it is to pick up women, right?"

"Somebody slap him upside the head for me."

Noah does the honor for me.

"Hey! What was that for? It's not a lie." Bode rubs the back of his head.

"Can you maybe not be such a sleaze all the time?" I scoff. "Maybe Jasper wants a connection with someone."

"Alright," Noah starts, "Marcus is happy. Jasper is

happy. Bode doesn't want a relationship if it were to smack him in the face. That leaves…"

"No." Dax starts shaking his head. "No way. I do not want you guys hooking me up."

"Why not? It's not like we'll let Bode set you up."

A weird look washes over his face. "I don't need you guys to set me up."

"See?" Jasper unpauses the game before him and Dax get back to it. "Everyone is happy."

Happy.

It's a foreign feeling. I mean, I'm happy with my life. I love Sam and Sadie. But the happiness of being with Harper? It's different.

Like it's something just for me.

Pulling out my phone, I let the guys go back to whatever conversation they're having and text Harper.

MARCUS

You make me happy, you know that?

HARPER

I do?

Yes.

Is there a reason you're telling me?

No point in hiding it

I don't want to screw up with you

Wow

An adult relationship. I like it 🩶

What can I say? I'm a single dad. No beating around the bush

Well, you make me happy

"SEE, THERE'S THAT SMILE AGAIN," Bode points out as Dax and Graham face off in the final round. "You really are in a good mood."

My phone buzzes again. This time, I see a photo come through. Before I open it, I wave my goodbyes.

"Since I lost, I'm heading down to bed. I'll see you guys tomorrow." I point to Jasper. "Your job to make sure they stay in line."

Jasper groans. "Fine."

Once I get out into the hallway, I head toward the elevator to get back down to my room. I pull up the picture Harper sent.

Fuck me.

She's wearing my jersey while blowing me a kiss.

HARPER

Thought this was good luck tonight

MARCUS

I've never looked so good

Damn right

You gonna wear that to your second game of the season?

Second? What makes you think I haven't been to more?

I SMILE to myself as I flick the room key over the lock and head inside. It's your run-of-the-mill hotel room. Nothing fancy. I've gotten used to them over the years. A place to rest my head on the road.

> Spill, Mrs. Evans

Mrs. Evans? Is that what you're calling me, Mr. Evans?

> Yes

You know I never changed my name, right?

> Are you trying to distract me from the question at hand?

🙄

> You forget I have twin girls

> I can spot a ruse a mile away

Fine. I went to the game in Vegas

MY THUMBS CAN'T MOVE FAST ENOUGH.

> The season opener? You were at the game in Vegas? Why? You hated me

🙄

> Again with the eye roll emoji

I didn't hate you

Really?

Well, one step up from hate

But once I knew the reason you left, it was hard to hate you

Logically going to the game was the next thing to do

As one does

That hockey fan is still buried in there

Sigh…she is

This means you have to come to a game

And not hide away

I'm definitely not going to the WAGs suite

I have seats for the girls

Maybe you can take them?

Really?

Would you want to?

Yes

Then it's a date

Well, you know what I mean

A family date

I can't wait

Chapter Twenty-Three

HARPER

Rain is coming down in sheets as a streak of lightning lights up the sky. Parking the car, I flip up my hood, grab my bag, and make a dash inside the open garage door where Marcus is waiting for me.

"Hi."

"It is gross out."

Marcus laughs, dropping a quick peck on my cheek. "Nice to see you too."

I fist his sweatshirt, pulling him back down. "Hi."

His lips are warm and sweet and taste like apples. When I step back, shaking the water off my coat, his eyes are lit up like the sky. How is this man so effortlessly sexy?

"The girls are excited to see you. They made you a sandwich."

"Grilled cheese and apples by chance?"

Marcus nods, taking my coat as we step inside the garage. A clap of thunder rings out. "Yes. Dinner is in the tent tonight."

"Tent?" I ask.

He points toward the living room. "Go see. The girls are waiting for you."

Toeing off my shoes, I head through the kitchen into the living room where a movie is playing on the TV. A pink tent, bigger than any tent I've seen, fills the space in front of it with both flaps open. The second Sam spots me, her face lights up.

"Harper! We made you dinner."

"I heard." I sit down and cross my legs in front of them.

Sam pats the spot next to her. "There's enough room for you in here."

"Daddy can fit too. We're having dinner in here tonight," Sadie tells me.

Sliding inside, it's bigger than it looks. Pillows and stuffed animals line the sides of the tent. Two sleeping bags lie on the floor.

"It's a party in here."

"Here's your dinner." Sadie hands me a plate of a gooey grilled cheese sandwich with carrots on the plate.

"Did you make this?" I settle the plate on my lap as Marcus manages to wedge himself in the tight space, shuffling a few animals around.

They both nod proudly. "Daddy helps," Sadie points out.

"But we put all the apples and cheese on," Sam says.

I take a bite. "It's delicious. My compliments to the chefs."

Marcus grins at me as he takes a bite of his own. The girls are beaming at me as they stuff their faces with their own sandwiches.

The storm rages outside as a boom of thunder shakes the house, causing Sadie to whimper and me to jump.

"I don't like storms," Sadie whispers, covering her ears.

"It's okay. I don't like storms either." Setting my empty plate outside of the tent, I pull Sadie onto my lap. "Is it because they're loud?"

She nods her head. "Yeah."

"Well, what's something we could do that's equally loud?"

"We could yell," Sam pipes up. "But Daddy says there's no yelling inside."

Another clap of thunder rings out, causing Sadie to burrow farther into my arms.

"I think I could make an exception this one time. But you know what I taught you girls?"

"What?" Sam asks, a confused look on her face.

Marcus leans down to whisper into Sam's ear and her face lights up. "Our favorite things!"

"Your what?" I ask. I surely couldn't have heard her right.

"Daddy says if you're scared of storms to think of your favorite things," Sadie turns around and tells me.

"And where did Daddy learn that?" I ask, looking at Marcus directly in his warm, brown eyes.

"I learned it from someone very smart," he says. "Kind of like your mom in that way."

"Our mom was really smart," Sadie tells me.

Marcus nods. "You know it's where you get your mad chess skills."

Sadie giggles. "I want to be a world champion."

"You can do anything you want, Sadie," Marcus tells her. "Your mom would love that."

I love that Marcus doesn't shy away from keeping the memory of their parents alive. Even though he is their Daddy, their biological mom and dad aren't hidden like a dirty topic.

This man. When he left, I put him and everything about our life together in a box and tucked it away. I didn't want to keep it, but I couldn't part with it for some reason. Now that he's back, I can't help but fall for him again.

Because even if I wasn't with him, I was still a part of his life. The small things that he did for me, he does for the girls. Even though Marcus left, it's like I never really left him.

"Tell me more of your favorite things," I tell the girls.

"I like macaroni and cheese and rainbows and unicorns and chess and reading," Sadie rattles off.

"Anything else?" Marcus asks with a grin.

"School. I like school."

"And puppies!" Sam chimes in, causing Marcus to groan.

"What's wrong with puppies?" I ask.

"We want a puppy and *Dad* won't get us one."

I try to hide the smile at the way she calls him Dad. Like this is the biggest grievance in their world that Marcus won't get them a dog.

"*Dad* doesn't have enough time for a puppy with hockey."

"But we'll take care of her," Sadie tells him, giving him a stern eye. "Trixie would be the best puppy ever."

"You already have her name picked out?" I ask the girls, and they both nod.

"From Bluey," Marcus says. "Always about Bluey."

"Bluey is not one of Daddy's favorite things," Sam says.

"You know what is one of my favorite things?"

Both their faces get excited at this. Clearly they know what one of his favorite things is.

"Ice cream!" they shout at the same time.

"Can we have some?" Sadie asks.

"Of course," Marcus says. "Harper, you want to help me?"

"Sure."

Marcus holds out his arm for me to lead the way out of the tent. From here, the girls can't see the kitchen, but the TV screen casts them in a glow. They've turned their attention to the movie playing.

"How are you holding up?" Marcus asks, opening the freezer and pulling out a gallon of strawberry ice cream.

I shrug a shoulder. "I guess spending storms with you isn't the worst place to be."

That earns me a laugh. "Do you need to tell me your favorite things?"

Draping my arms over Marcus's shoulders, I pull him close.

"You."

"It seems like we have the same favorite things because you're my favorite thing too." Marcus buries his face into my neck and I'm swept away in his warmth. In how safe I feel with him.

I don't know how long we stay like this, just breathing each other in. I always remember passing the storms with Marcus in my apartment. We'd pull the blankets up over our heads and talk for hours.

Those are the things I missed most. Now I'm doing it with Marcus and his girls, which I love.

"Is the ice cream ready yet?" Sam calls out.

"In a minute," Marcus tells them.

I laugh into him, squeezing the back of his neck. "I guess they won't wait for their ice cream."

"Can't say that I blame them."

We scoop ice cream into bowls for the four of us as the storm starts to settle outside. The girls have a lantern lit up inside of the tent as they each tell us their own stories they made up.

"Daddy, can we have a sleepover down here?" Sadie asks around a yawn.

"Why else do you think we brought the sleeping bags down?" he asks them. "I think it's time to tuck in and go to bed."

"Can we watch Bluey when we wake up?" Sam asks.

Marcus nods. "Yes. And maybe we can make pancakes tomorrow morning."

Sadie's eyes go wide. "But it's not Sunday."

"Well, maybe Harper can come for breakfast—"

"Yes!" they both answer immediately, cutting Marcus off.

"I think this is a great idea," I tell them.

Marcus gives them each a kiss as I hug them good night.

"Night, girls."

"Night!"

Zipping the tent up for them, I link hands with Marcus as he leads me upstairs.

"Ready for our own sleepover?"

"More than ready."

WELCOME
TO Fabulous
LAS VEGA
NEVADA

Chapter Twenty-Four

MARCUS

"God, I've missed you."

Lifting Harper into my arms, I carry her up the stairs. The rain is quieter now. I know the girls will sleep through the night with the sounds of the TV on downstairs. Which means I can have Harper all to myself.

"We talked every day you were gone," Harper tells me.

"But I didn't get to see you."

I shut my bedroom door behind me—making sure to lock it—before resting both of us in the center of the bed.

"Tell me something no one else knows about you."

"You know everything." Harper smiles up at me.

I shake my head, pulling her closer to me. We're on our sides facing one another. I push a leg through hers, wrapping her leg over mine so we're tangled together. Resting my hands on her waist, I drop my forehead to hers.

Breathing her in.

"Not everything. I want to know everything that happened to you these last few years."

"Nothing significant happened to me. No broken

bones. No new house. A new job is about the only thing that changed about me."

"That's it?" I tuck a lock of hair behind her ear, trailing my thumb along her jaw. "Nothing else happened?"

Harper presses a kiss to the corner of my mouth. "I missed you. I tried not to, but every time I thought I was over you, something would happen—something small—and it would remind me of you. I hated it. Hated that I still wished I could have you."

"You know why I don't really drink?" I ask her.

"Why not?"

I sigh. "There was one night when the girls were two maybe. Sadie had a raging fever and Sam wouldn't settle down. My mom was with me that night because I had a game, but when I got home, neither of them would settle down. Even with the two of us, I think I got maybe an hour of sleep? I was rocking with Sadie and, in a moment of weakness, looked at your social media. You were with some guy."

"Really?" Harper questions.

I nod. "I was so upset that I got wasted after Sadie finally fell asleep. The next morning, her fever got worse and I needed to take her to the hospital. I was so miserable, I had to have my mom take her and I stayed home with Sam."

"You know that's not your fault, right?" Harper whispers.

"It felt like it. I let them down and I never want to do that."

"You know there was never anyone serious, right? I don't think I could have ever made room for anyone but you."

"I wish I could go back and change things, Harper."

"I know you do. But we can't change the past. We can only move forward."

A smile tugs at the corner of my mouth. "Into the future. You and me."

"Yeah. Me and you."

I capture her lips with mine. A hard, deep kiss that pours out every ounce of emotion I'm feeling for this woman right now. Hell, emotions I've always felt—love and adoration for her.

Flipping us over so she's on her back, I link our hands together and pull them above her head.

"Marcus." There's a sexy rasp to her voice.

"I can't wait to have my way with you tonight, Harper."

"You can have me any way you want."

Rocking back onto my hips, I tug the sweater she's wearing up and over her head. Her nipples are tight through her bra as I let my eyes drink her in.

I didn't get to do this last time. I was too desperate for her and had to have her. Tonight, I am going to take my time. There is no rush to go anywhere. No need to be back home.

Just the two of us.

"You are so fucking sexy, Harper." I drag a finger over the black cup of her bra. "The way you drive me crazy."

"Not as crazy as you make me."

I kiss my way down Harper's body, stripping her of all her clothes. By the time I'm throwing her underwear over my shoulder, I'm dizzy with lust.

All this beautiful, naked skin laid out before me. I can't wait to get my mouth on her.

I nibble and lick her leg, taking my time. Each nip and suck is making my dick rock hard. The mewls and purrs from Harper make this so much more fun.

By the time I make it to her pussy, I can see her need. She's dripping.

"Do you know how sexy you are when you want me like this?"

"I need you, Marcus. Oh God, please."

Her begs are a balm to my soul as I kiss her everywhere except where she really wants me. She's writhing beneath me. Setting a hand on her stomach, I hold her down.

"Patience, Harper."

"Go faster," Harper groans.

Peeking one eye up at her, I grin when I see her hands are covering her face.

"Not a chance. I want to savor every drop." I flick her clit with my tongue, the softest move designed to tease her. "Mmm, so fucking good."

"You are infuriating!"

Putting her out of her misery, I run my tongue through her wet folds. I devour her as I listen to the praise she's heaping on me.

I spread her legs as I eat her pussy. Harper's hands sink into my hair, clutching the strands with a firm grip.

"I'm going to come."

"Yes. Let me taste you, baby." I suck on her clit again, flicking it with my tongue before thrusting it back inside her.

"Gah!" Harper comes on a cry. I take everything she is giving me, drinking down every trace of her orgasm.

"So fucking perfect."

Her body is spent. I crawl up her and fuse my lips onto hers. She's needy, chasing my tongue with hers.

Fuck. She's not the only one. After seeing her come, tasting her release, I need to be inside her.

"On your stomach."

Standing, I shuck the rest of my clothes and grab a

condom from the nightstand. Harper's eyes rake over my body, stopping as I stroke my cock. "See what you do to me?"

"Why don't you let me feel what I do to you…" she fires back.

"Careful, or I might not let you," I chuckle.

Except I don't want to keep teasing her. I want to be balls deep inside of her more than anything. Pushing her legs together, I drop mine on the outside of her thighs and pull her hips up.

Harper's heels dig into my ass as I slide into the tight heat of her pussy. Made even tighter as I squeeze her legs together.

Fuck. I have to take a few deep breaths so I don't come immediately. "How do you feel so damn amazing?"

"It's only because it's you," Harper purrs.

Leaning over her back, I grab her chin and plant a kiss on her lips. Even buried inside her warmth, I can't resist touching her everywhere. The desire to be closer, connected, drives me wild.

Fuck. Being with Harper like this is everything.

"Perfect, babe. So sweet. So perfect. Absolutely fucking perfect."

"Fuck me, Marcus," Harper breathes against my lips.

"Gladly."

I set a punishing pace. Her pussy squeezes my cock to within an inch of its life. Pleasure snakes through me as I pump my hips inside her.

The pressure builds as I keep moving. It's pure bliss being with Harper. "God damn. You feel fucking amazing."

"So do you. Your cock. It's…"

"It's what?" I push Harper's hair to the side and nibble on her earlobe. "Tell me."

"Perfect. It's the perfect size. I love the way you fit inside me."

I thrust again, letting her feel my full length. "It's like you were made just for me."

"Only for you."

"Hell yes, baby."

I can't hold back any longer. My hips are moving at a frantic speed, needing to get both of us off now. When Harper starts to come again, it only takes two more thrusts before I'm emptying my release into the condom.

"Fuck," I growl. "Fuck!"

Holding her hips, I let the pleasure wash through me.

It's unreal. Every minute of tonight has been unreal. Because I'm here with Harper.

Pulling out, I tie off the condom and take it into the bathroom before heading back to the bed. She hasn't moved. Her eyes are closed, a happy smile firmly in place.

"You good?" I drag a finger down her back.

Harper peeks one eye open at me. "I'll be even better once you get into bed with me."

Shifting Harper so I can pull the sheets over us, I tuck her into my side. "I can't wait to do that again."

"And again," Harper echoes.

Until then, I'm going to hold her in my arms and never let go.

WELCOME
TO Fabulous
LAS VEGAS
NEVADA

Chapter Twenty-Five

MARCUS

"**A**re you sure it's a good idea I spend the night?" Harper asks, not for the first time.

"How many times do I need to tell you it's okay?" I shake my head at her.

"I don't want this to cause any problems for the girls."

I press a kiss to the crown of her head. After another round, we're lying in bed together, perfectly content. The rain has picked up again, beating a heavy pattern against the windows.

"You won't."

"How do you know?" Harper pops her head up, looking me dead in the eye. "Are they ready to see you with a woman?"

I smile at her, fingering a soft strand of her hair. "They've already seen us together."

"But not like this," Harper clarifies.

"You are the only person I want them to see me with. They love you. I love you. It's not—"

"You love me?" Harper cuts me off.

"I thought that was fairly obvious."

"It's not too fast?"

I shake my head. "Considering I'm still your husband…"

Harper laughs out loud, covering her mouth before looking toward the door.

"Don't worry." I pull her hand off her mouth and kiss her. "They won't hear you."

"You know, we never really did get around to filing those divorce papers."

"Is that something you'd like to get around to doing?" I ask, holding my breath.

Is this the time to be asking this question? Probably not. Not with her here in my arms, fully sated after a few orgasms.

But I need to know.

"If I did, then I'd miss this."

"Miss what?" I bring her hand to my lips and kiss the palm.

"Lying in bed together. Cuddling with you."

"I do love cuddling with you."

"See? I'd miss out on this side of you that I love so much."

Flipping her over, I settle my weight on top of her. All of that blonde hair spills across my pillow like strands of gold.

"That you love so much?"

Harper smirks at me. "I thought that was fairly obvious."

This time it's me who's bursting out with laughter. "God, I love you, Harper."

"Not as much as I love you, Marcus."

Her big, blue eyes are bright and full of love. I give her a soft, slow kiss. Sweet. Nothing heated.

"So that divorce then…"

Harper threads her fingers through my hair, brushing it from my forehead. "Eh, I'm kind of attached to my husband."

I can't hide my smile. It's the one that Harper was always able to pull from me so easily.

"It feels kind of weird," I tell her.

"Being married?"

I nod. "We got married, were told it wasn't real, spent seven years apart only to realize it's actually legitimate. Who knew?"

"Maybe it means we need to do something to celebrate it actually being real."

"You know who's going to want to help with that?"

Harper smiles. "The girls."

I nod. "The girls. Which means we should probably tell them we're dating."

"Only dating?"

"Ease them into it. I don't think Sam and Sadie need to know our entire history right this very minute."

"You're right." Harper sits up, covering her chest with the bedsheet. "We can tell them how we met in college when they're older."

"When you accosted me at a pep rally."

"Excuse me!" Harper slaps my chest. "I did not."

"I mean, you were pretty forceful in getting through that group of women to get to me."

"Well, what can I say." She smiles. "When I see what I want, I go after it."

"Same. And right now, all I want is you."

Harper kisses me. "Right now, all I want is something to eat. As much as I love you, if we're going to do this again—"

"If? There's no question. I want at least one more orgasm out of you tonight, Harper." I kiss her and hop out of bed. "Stay put. I'll grab us some snacks so the girls don't wake up."

Based on her reaction, she's not paying attention to me at all. I grab the gray sweats I was wearing earlier and slip them on.

"I'll be right back." I wink at her as she grabs the TV remote.

"Hurry." Her eyes are hungry for me.

I'm fast and quiet as I head downstairs. Checking on the girls, they're sound asleep. I turn off the TV and lower the overhead lights so it's not completely dark for them.

I grab a bag of chips, some veggies, and two waters for us before rushing back upstairs.

I don't want to keep Harper waiting.

When I sneak back inside, she's wearing my T-shirt and has an episode of Bluey on.

"Really? You're watching this too?"

Harper is grinning like a fool at me. "Oh no. I turned the TV on and it was playing already."

"That's because the girls were watching it in here."

"Were they?" Harper quirks a brow at me. "Or are you a secret Bluey fan and don't let anyone know it?"

"Crap."

"Oh my God. You do love this show!"

Setting the food down between us, I hand her a water. "Who doesn't love this show? I had to see what happened when they thought they were moving."

"Okay." Harper opens the bag of carrots and crunches one in half. "Then why do the girls think you don't like this show?"

I sigh, grabbing my own carrot. "If they knew, we'd never watch it. When I start liking their shows, they tell me they aren't cool anymore and don't want to watch them."

Harpers laughs, covering her mouth. "They are going to be such a handful as teenagers."

"Don't remind me."

"I'm really digging Daddy Marcus."

"Oh my God, stop."

"What? You don't like it when I call you *daddy*?"

I shake my head. "Not when the girls call me that."

"This is going to be such good blackmail."

"I can't with you." I shake my head and open the chips and pop one in my mouth. "There is no need for blackmail. No one needs to know about my secret love of Bluey."

"It's a good thing you love me." Harper is gloating and loving every minute of what she learned.

"I don't know why. Now, finish your snacks because I'm going to punish you for being a bad girl."

"I've been a bad girl?" She quirks a brow at me.

"Yes. No making fun of me when I'm feeding you and giving you orgasms."

"Duly noted." Harper gives me a salute before shoving a handful of chips in her mouth. She looks like the cutest fucking chipmunk on the planet like that. God, I really don't know how I lived without her.

I love this woman and I will do everything in my power to make sure I keep her this time.

Harper and the girls are all I could ever possibly need in life. I lost her once, and I sure as hell am not going to lose her again.

Because Harper's it.

WELCOME
TO
Fabulous
LAS VEGAS
NEVADA

Chapter Twenty-Six

There's a happy ache in my body as sunlight filters in through the curtains. A soft breath blows across my chest as limbs start moving.

Damn. I could get used to this.

Waking up with Harper in my arms? Not sure if life could get any better.

"Are you awake?" I whisper.

"It's too early."

"Morning, sunshine."

Harper groans, rolling away from me and burying her face in the pillow that she didn't use, opting to use me as one instead.

"You're still not a morning person?"

"I'm a morning person five days out of the week, Marcus. I like being able to sleep in every now and then."

"Weekends are not made for sleeping in around here." I press a kiss between her shoulder blades. "If you want, you can go back to sleep, and I can get started on breakfast with the girls."

Harper rolls back over, a smile peeking out from the

mess of hair hiding her face. "I mean, I guess I could wake up for breakfast. As long as it's pancakes."

"Take your time."

Harper pops up, hair a complete mess. That has a smug smile spreading across my face because the memories of last night are still very fresh in my mind.

"Won't the girls wonder why I'm here?"

"Do you want to tell them?" I ask, grabbing a hoodie from my dresser and pulling it on.

"Isn't that kind of a big step?" she asks.

"Bigger than saying I love you last night?" I waggle my eyebrows at her.

"I mean, don't get me wrong, I love the girls, but I don't want to—"

"You're overthinking this," I interrupt, walking over to press a kiss to the worry lines in her forehead. "I'm all in, Harper. Whether we tell the girls now or later, that's not going to change."

A happy sigh escapes her. "I'm all in too, Marcus. I've been all in on you since day one. I mean, I guess we can tell them."

"You guess?" I ask her.

"Okay, fine, we can tell them. Should we wait and go downstairs until they're awake?"

I shake my head. "They're already awake."

Harper looks at the clock on my bedside table. "It's only seven."

"And I promised them pancakes. They're up. Besides, I heard the TV on downstairs." Harper throws the comforter back and I don't hide the way I watch her as she covers her gorgeous body in a pair of yoga pants and one of my sweatshirts. "Now get that cute ass of yours downstairs."

As soon as my bottom foot hits the first floor, I take

Harper's hand and give it a squeeze. I know she's anxious about telling the girls about us, but I know they'll love it. Sam and Sadie love their nanny, and I know they'll love Harper just as much. They need a strong, female influence in their life. I know Harper will be it for them, and she'll love being there for them.

"Harper." Sam spots her right away and jumps off the couch to give her a hug. "Why are you over so early?"

The tent is abandoned as each girl sits in their spot on the couch with, no surprise, Bluey on TV.

"I heard all about this pancake breakfast, so I had to come over for it."

Sadie comes over to give Harper a hug too. "Do you have a bad joke to tell?"

Harper squats down on their level. "It's not Sunday. I thought bad jokes were only for Sundays."

Both girls shake their heads. "We have two really good jokes to tell."

"I can't wait to hear them." Harper is beaming at them. "I have one too."

"Yes." Sadie pumps her fist.

"Before breakfast, Harper and I have something to tell you," I say.

"Can we finish this episode?" Sam asks.

I grab the remote from the end table and pause it. "You've seen it a hundred times. We can watch it after breakfast."

Sadie eyes me, assessing me. Girl is too smart for her own good. "If we listen really good, can we both have chocolate chips then?"

Why is everything always a bargaining chip with kids?

"You can both have chocolate chips if you listen well," Harper answers for me.

"Hey, aren't I supposed to make that decision?"

Harper stands back up, resting her hands on her hips. "What, like you were going to say no to them?"

The girls giggle as they each take their seat on the couch. "Hurry up because I'm hungry," Sadie says.

"Well, you know how Harper and I have been spending time together?" I ask them.

"Yeah." Sadie nods.

"Harper and I really like each other, so we're dating."

"Do you loooove each other?" Sam giggles.

Sadie laughs next to her. "Eww. Do you kiss?"

"Christ," I mutter to myself, scrubbing a hand down my face. "Where did you learn about that?"

"Bobby at school said if two adults like each other, they kiss," Sadie says, matter-of-factly.

"No more hanging out with Bobby."

"Bobby's a good kid," Harper says. "You're just mad because they know what it is."

I point to both girls. "No kissing any boys. Especially that Bobby."

"Does that mean you kiss Harper?" Sadie asks. "If you love each other, you can kiss."

"I guess that means we do love each other," Harper says, looking at me. There's nothing but love shining through her eyes.

I can't help myself. I give Harper the shortest, softest, sweetest kiss ever.

"Gross," both girls say.

"Now." I want to make this point before I lose them. "While Harper is here, you can call her Harper, but if you see her at school, I want you to call her Miss Smith, okay? The other kids don't need to be calling her Harper."

"Okay," Sam says. "Can we have pancakes now?"

"Yes, time for pancakes," I tell them.

"If Harper comes over, will Gigi still come play with us?" Sadie asks, following Sam into the kitchen and pulling out the bag of chocolate chips. I don't miss her sneaking a few in her mouth.

"She will." I take the bag from her so it won't be gone before breakfast is made.

Broaching the subject of Harper with my mom is a topic for a different day. Without the ears of little girls around. It's not one I'm looking forward to. Telling the truth to my mom about what happened all those years ago isn't going to be easy. There's a lot of hurt to overcome, but maybe if she sees the two of us are in this for the long haul, it won't matter.

Breakfast is a happy affair. The girls pepper Harper with questions that she asks them right back. Fuck, I don't know if I've ever been this happy in my life.

"You said we can watch this episode of Bluey," Sadie tells me after she clears her plate. "One episode, please?"

"Look how sad they look," Harper whispers. "You have to tell them you like this show."

"You like Bluey?" Sam pops up from behind me. "You said you didn't like Bluey."

"Oops." Harper is smiling too widely for her own good.

"You set me up for that."

"I did no such thing." She throws her hands up in defense.

"You so did." I drop the plates in the sink and stride around the counter to where Harper is sitting on the stool.

"Oh yeah? What are you going to do about it?"

"Get her, girls."

Sam and Sadie need no further prompting as we all start tickling Harper. It's the best punishment I can give her right now as her laughter mixes with the girls' and echoes throughout the house.

I'm becoming a sap, because hearing and seeing these three together is about the best damn thing in the world. Getting to wake up to this every weekend?

Yeah, I could get used to it.

WELCOME
TO
Fabulous
LAS VEGAS
NEVADA

"Hard to believe the holidays are coming up," Noah tells me.

These last few weeks have flown by. It's gone by in a blur of events with the girls, nights with Harper, and hockey games.

So many games.

With the holiday season upon us, my mom will be home soon and it will be time to break the news to her that Harper and I are together. I'm surprised the girls haven't told her yet on their calls. But with chess being Sadie's thing, she loves talking about that more.

Thank God.

If Emma isn't with the girls, it's Harper. I even gave her extra booster seats for the girls so she could have them in case of an emergency.

Harper's done more than just have them in case of an emergency. She's taken them to pottery classes on the weekend when I have games. Movies when I have an extra practice. Tucking them in and reading them books.

At this point, I'm not sure who they love more—me or Harper.

"Are you heading back home to Denver?" I ask Noah.

"Nah. Family is coming here. We wanted to spend our first Christmas together in our new place. What about you?"

"We'll be spending it here before the girls visit Dan's parents."

"That'll be fun for them."

"They always have a good time."

A few times throughout the year, the girls will take a week or two and go visit my brother-in-law's parents. I hate that they live in Washington, but with them being older, it's harder for them to come visit the girls. I wish they could see them more, but the girls still love them. I know they're looking forward to another Christmas with them. Especially because they have a new dog.

One of these days, I'm going to cave and get them a dog. It's only a matter of time.

"You boys ready for warm-ups?" Bode asks, walking by us to head out to the rink.

"Just finishing up."

Grabbing my phone, I see one last text from Harper. Since it's an early afternoon game, she's bringing the girls with her.

A photo of all three of them in front of the arena awaits me—with each of them wearing my jersey. The girls are wearing their Knights hats and look fucking adorable.

> **HARPER**
>
> Good luck! We'll be cheering loud for you 🖤

The girls said if you score a goal, they get
a dog

I SHAKE MY HEAD LAUGHING.

"The girls?" Jasper asks as he and I head out.

"Yeah. Apparently if I score tonight, they get a dog."

Jasper chuckles as we hit the ice. "I'll score for you then."

"What a martyr you are."

We're still a good hour away from the puck dropping, but the arena is packed. With the Black Diamonds in town, tickets were at a premium. Both teams are playing well this year, and it could be an indicator of the playoffs.

"Are you really not going to say hi to me?" the familiar voice calls out on the ice during warm-ups.

Skating over to the Colorado zone, I see my best friend from my college playing days, Troy Hollins, standing there shaking his head.

"Hey, I'm not getting in between any man and his pregame rituals."

Troy pulls me in for a quick hug. "I can't believe you didn't tell me."

"I'm surprised I didn't get a call chewing me out."

"And miss ripping you a new one in person? Why didn't you tell me?"

Troy was one of my closest friends in college. His wife, Angie? Harper's best friend. When shit hit the fan, I cut off all contact. It doesn't surprise me that he now knows the truth about what happened.

"Wasn't exactly something I was proud of."

"You know I would have been there for you, right?" Troy tells me. Hurt laces his voice.

"I could barely be there for the girls. I'm sorry, man. If I could take it back, I would." I bump him on the shoulder. "But I know congratulations are in order for you. I hear Angie is due anytime?"

"Guess I'll be calling you for parenting advice."

"I don't know. The girls said they get a dog if I score tonight." I laugh.

Troy skates away from me. "I'll make sure you don't get a dog then."

"Are you trying to goad me into scoring?"

"Not with Nick on goal!"

I go back to my end of the ice, watching as Noah chats with a few of the guys. Since he used to play for Colorado before he got traded, he knows the guys better.

If there's one thing I want tonight, it's to wipe the ice with the Black Diamonds. We beat them last season, and I'd love to do it again. They're one of the best teams in the league, and with our schedule this year, it would prove that we're not a circled win anymore. That teams won't look at the schedule before the season starts and assume they're winning against us.

All niceties between the teams are forgotten as soon as the puck drops. Colorado skates hard during the first period to put two points on the scoreboard.

With Brooks-Young in goal, he's stopping everything we're sending his way. But by the time the second period starts, we finally get our shot.

Dax takes off down the ice and I'm right behind him. The only person in our way is one of their defensemen. With some quick stick work, Dax fires the puck back to me and I'm sending it sailing into the back of the net.

I'm laughing as the guys come over to congratulate me. I can hear the cheers now. *We're getting a dog!*

"Why are you shaking your head that you scored?" Bode asks as we skate back to the bench.

"Two little girls think they're getting a dog now."

Bode cackles. Full on cackles at that, the fucker. "They are so getting a dog."

"They are not."

I take my seat on the bench and swig from my water bottle as the game starts up again.

"Cap, you are whipped. You would do anything for them. Whether it's now or in a few months, the girls are getting a dog."

Damn it. They really are.

I can't say no to them. And if they get Harper on their side? It's a done deal.

I turn my focus back to the game. We've tied it up by the time we get into the third period, but then Bode gets a lucky shot through the goalie's legs.

When the final horn sounds, we put Colorado away, 3-2.

"Sorry, man," I tell Troy as we shake hands after the game.

"I feel sorry for you. Good luck with that dog." He laughs.

"I'm going to get two and send one your way."

"If it means you bring it out and come see us, I'm all for it."

I nod at him. "You got it."

"I'm serious." Troy pulls me in for a hug. "Once the baby comes, come visit. I miss you, man."

"I miss you too."

For playing against him through the years, he did a good job ignoring me on the ice. Not that I sought him out either.

"Have a safe trip home," I tell him.

"See ya, man."

I head back to the locker room for the usual post-game routine.

Talking with media and recapping the game. A quick shower and changing back into my gameday suit.

A text is waiting for me.

> I'm supposed to tell you that you scored and you know what that means

It doesn't mean anything

> Do you really want to disappoint these faces?

A PICTURE of both girls eating hot dogs comes through. Ketchup rings their mouths. I smile at their happy faces.

Don't encourage them

> They are planning on discussing this with you when you get home

About that

> Yeah?

Want to spend the night together?

> What about the girls?

"HEY." I elbow Noah in the side as he's getting ready to leave. "Any chance you and Graham would want to spend the night with the girls?"

"What's in it for us?" Graham asks before Noah can even respond.

"Hanging with two girls that love you?"

"They'd love us regardless."

"Fine," I groan. "I'll buy the next round of drinks when we go out."

"Done," Graham agrees.

"You're lucky I love you," Noah tells him. "We'll be there in an hour. Does that work?"

"Perfect."

> Noah and Graham are going to watch them.

I'll order dinner and pick it up once I drop the girls off

> Hopefully Noah and Graham won't take too long

I'll just be waiting for you all sad and lonely at my place

Whatever shall I do to pass the time 😌

"I APPRECIATE YOU GUYS."

"You won't when we're drinking on your tab." Noah slaps me on the shoulder as he and Graham head out.

It's a balancing act, life as a single dad. Between the girls and hockey, and now Harper, it feels like someone is always going to get the short end of the stick. Learning to lean on people has never been easy for me. But these guys? I guess I can learn to trust people.

Getting to show up for Harper? I want to be that man for her. To let her know that she can trust me. That I won't run this time.

That I'm here for good.

Chapter Twenty-Eight

"I hope you still like Thai."

Glancing at Marcus over the island in my kitchen, my heart rate picks up. He's handsome, if a little disheveled after his game. His gaze droops from exhaustion as he rounds the counter with one aim in mind.

Me.

"After a game, I'll eat anything." Marcus steals a kiss from me before heading toward my living room. "But you know Pad Thai is the key to my heart."

"Is it?" I grab my own plastic container of fried rice and follow Marcus, sitting next to him. "Good to know."

It's a tight squeeze on my love seat, but it's the only thing that fits in my small apartment.

"As long as I'm fed after a game, I'm happy."

Marcus is not shy at how fast he wolfs down his dinner. I'm not even halfway done by the time he's dropping the empty container on my coffee table and grabbing his water bottle.

"Do you want some of mine?" I hold the container out to him.

"Nah, I'm good. That was fucking delicious."

"You worked up quite the appetite," I observe.

"There are other ways I can work up an appetite…"

"Oh yeah?" Marcus grabs my foot and digs his fingers into the arch. "That feels amazing. Shouldn't you be the one that needs this after the game?"

"You rubbing me down?" Marcus waggles his eyebrows at me.

"I mean, yeah. But I won't say no to a foot rub."

I set my half-eaten dinner on the table and stretch both legs into Marcus's lap as best I can.

"You should know by now I won't say no to you."

"You mean anything I want, you'll say yes to?"

Marcus smiles. "Yes."

"What if I want a dog?"

That earns me a boisterous laugh. "Okay, fine. Within reason."

"And here I thought I was going to be Sam and Sadie's favorite person."

Marcus grabs my hand and presses a kiss to my palm. "You already are. Mine too."

"Wow." I laugh. "It was easy to win over the Evans family."

"You know, you're technically a part of it too."

Moving to straddle his lap, I run my fingers through his soft locks. "That's going to take some getting used to still."

"Anything I can do to help?"

"Oh, I don't know. I think you're doing it just by being here."

Marcus smiles at me, rubbing his thumb over my jaw. His fingers sink into my hair, massaging my scalp. "You're wearing an Evans jersey. I think that solidifies it. Especially with how damn sexy you look right now."

"I thought you might enjoy it."

"It means you're going to need to come to every game now and wear this. You're my good luck charm."

I wiggle over his lap, feeling his cock harden beneath me. "Could other things be considered a good luck charm?"

"What do you have in mind?"

Grabbing the hem of the jersey, I pull it up and over my head and unfasten my bra and flick that off. I make quick work of the buttons on his shirt and push it over his shoulders.

"I could get used to this." Marcus leans forward, closing his lips over my nipple.

The way he flicks his tongue over the tight bud has me arching into his hold. His large hands send fire pulsing through every inch of my body.

Pulling his mouth off me, I kiss him. Deep and fierce. Controlling it as he holds me close. Bare chest to bare chest. The contact is creating a storm of electricity around us. Our slow, languid kisses as our hands roam over each other ratchet up my desire.

I cannot get enough as I rock over him.

"Fuck, Harper. I cannot get enough of you," Marcus echoes my thoughts.

Standing, I grab his hand and pull him up with me. "Care to join me in the shower?"

I shimmy out of my leggings and toss them in Marcus's direction. He's tripping over himself to get his shoes and pants off, and laughter bubbles out of me.

By the time I flip the handle to start the shower, Marcus is behind me, pulling me into his arms. I lock eyes with him in the mirror.

My breath catches in my throat at the look on his face.

Desire. Want. More love than I ever thought I could have in this world.

"I fucking love you," Marcus whispers. His hands are resting on my hips, steam filling the bathroom. "More than I'll ever be able to tell you, Harper."

Pulling Marcus's hand to my mouth, I kiss the vein on his wrist. It's hard to contain the emotions that are swimming through me.

Love. Intimacy. Contentment. Trust.

"I love you forever and a day."

"Forever and a day," Marcus repeats back to me. "It won't be long enough."

"Then we better make good use of every minute we have."

Pushing the curtain back, I step into the shower and Marcus follows. His big frame takes the brunt of the water as he takes me into his arms and kisses me again. Water sluices over both our bodies as he spins me toward the cold, tiled wall. I wrap a leg around his hips to hold him close.

To feel exactly what I'm doing to him.

"Turn around. I'll wash your hair." A sly smile is on Marcus's face as I obey him. He snaps the shampoo bottle open and rubs some between his hands. Strong fingers work their magic as they massage it into my scalp.

"God, Marcus."

"Let me take care of you."

Tears sting my eyes at his words. I can't remember the last time someone took care of me. I've been on my own for so long, that it became my status quo.

Oil change? I learned to do it myself.

Hanging shelves? I'm a master at wielding a hammer.

Self-defense classes to stay safe on my own.

Marcus's words mean more to me than he'll ever know.

As he rinses the soap from my hair, he presses kisses into my shoulders. "Are you okay?"

I spin in his arms. "Yeah. I'm good. Perfect, actually."

Marcus brushes back the hair that sticks to my face and kisses me. Sweet, deep, *perfect*. Everything about this moment is perfect.

Marcus is all I will ever need in life. All I've ever needed.

"Let me take care of you."

Marcus shakes his head. "You don't have to."

I smile at him as I drop to my knees. "I want to. Let me."

"I love you," he tells me again, brushing his thumb over my lips.

I swirl my tongue around the head of his cock. Precum is already leaking out. I work my hand and mouth in tandem as I feel him harden.

"Do you realize how sexy you look right now?"

I smile as Marcus threads his fingers through my hair, guiding my moves. My free hand cups his balls as I tease him. Every groan of his is music to my ears. His broad shoulders block most of the water from hitting me. Drops of water slide down his sexy Adonis belt.

"Want me to come?" Marcus asks, his voice raspy with need.

I pull off him with a pop. "I want you to come down my throat."

"Fuck. Yes."

I suck him as far back as I can as I squeeze his balls, urging him to come. I love the taste of him. The feel. I tighten my fist right before he explodes. I swallow the salty cum of his orgasm. His growls and muttered *fucks* spur me on, feeding my desire to take every inch of him until he's shaking. Wanting to drink up every last drop. Loving that I can make him feel this way.

Lust-filled eyes stare down at me as he wiggles a finger

at me. As I stand, Marcus sweeps me into his arms and
plants a kiss on my lips.

"Now, let me take you to bed and show you how much
I love you. All night, love."

"Sounds perfect."

Chapter Twenty-Nine

HARPER

Hey, I'm going to be a little late from practice today. Would you mind taking the girls home? Emma is sick

Sure, I can do that

You're a lifesaver.

They have chess practice in the library

I owe you

I can think of a few ways you can pay me back...

Damn it, Harper. I'm at practice

I can't have this problem

Well, then I guess you're going to have to make it up to me tonight 😈

You're evil

. . .

I laugh, grabbing my purse from my desk and tucking my phone into it. I gather up my lesson plans and papers, hiding them away in my desk for tomorrow. Being ahead has its perks. Instead of having to worry about them tonight, I can spend the time with the girls.

Before, I would have spent all night working on my plans. It was all I would do during the week. I had the occasional nights out with friends, but school always came first.

Since Marcus came back into my life, it feels like I actually have one now.

Heading toward the library, I peek through the windows and watch the remainder of chess practice. A few students are gathered around Sadie and another boy who are playing one another. They're both concentrating hard, but I know the moment the move comes to Sadie. Her face lights up and she's moving her piece with easy confidence.

The two of them shake hands and I know she's won.

That's my girl.

Damn it. I don't need to be thinking of them like that. They're not mine. Marcus has always meant so much to me, but now, so do his girls. Marcus and I fell into this thing between the two of us so easily, that I'm waiting for the other shoe to drop.

I handled the heartbreak once. I don't know if I could do it again.

Shaking off the thoughts, I head into the library to watch the end of practice.

"Hey, Harper."

"Hi, Max," I greet the fifth-grade teacher who is in charge of the club. "I'm taking the girls home tonight."

"I just saw the email come through."

"Miss Smith! I won!" Sadie comes bolting over to me, jumping up and down with excitement. "I haven't beat a fifth grader yet."

"Did you tell him it was a good game?"

She nods, hair spilling out of her ponytail. "I did. We shook hands."

"Good job." An idea comes to mind. "What do you say we get ice cream on the way home to celebrate your big win?"

"Ice cream?" Sam comes over, threading her arms through her backpack straps. "We never get ice cream on the way home from school."

"I think we can make an exception with Sadie's big win."

"Okay!"

"And then maybe we can make dinner together so it's ready when Dad gets home?"

"Best day ever!" Sadie grabs Sam's hand and they run off toward the lobby of the school.

I wave to Max as I chase after them.

"Slow down, girls."

I grab their hands as I steer them toward my car. With Marcus's mom being gone, I got an extra set of booster seats.

Just in case.

I've ended up using them more than I thought I would. It's like Marcus knew he would need me. I like that he can rely on me. Anything for him and the girls.

But I don't mind. Making sure they're strapped in, I hop into the driver's seat and start the car.

"Tell me about this winning chess move," I say to Sadie.

There's a small mom-and-pop ice cream shop a few

miles from the school, but with traffic, it's taking us a while to get there.

"He thought he had me with his queen, but I saw a move with my bishop and I was able to take it. After that, it was an easy checkmate."

"Is that the one you used to beat me?"

"Yes."

"Well, I'm not very good, but I'm glad you won."

"I was able to capture seven pieces," Sam tells me. "I usually don't get that many."

"Good job, Sam. Looks like we'll have two chess wizards to contend with."

"She did a really good job," Sadie agrees.

I smile, inching our way toward our destination. I like that these two have each other. Sam might not like chess all that much, but she plays so she can spend the time with Sadie. My older sister and I were never that close when we were younger. We are now, but we still don't get to see each other that often since she lives in California.

The girls are chattering about their day as the arrow lights up. The car in front of me goes, but the next thing I know, the sound of squealing brakes hits me. I have less than a second to throw my arm out before the air bags explode.

Holy shit.

The smell of smoke is thick in the small car as my ears ring.

Sam and Sadie. It's the only thought that penetrates my rattled brain as I turn to find them screaming in the backseat.

"Are you okay?"

Sam is crying and Sadie has her eyes squeezed shut with her hands over her ears. They're both frazzled, but at first glance, they look okay.

Holy shit. There's a dull throbbing in my head, and my wrist aches.

"It's okay, girls. It'll be okay."

I'm saying it as much to them as I am to myself.

"I want Daddy," Sam cries. "Where's Daddy?"

Marcus.

Oh God. We were in an accident. He's going to hate me. Knowing everything that happened to his sister, he is going to hate me.

I try to take a few deep breaths so I don't lose it in front of the girls.

"I'm scared, Harper," Sadie tells me.

"I know, sweetheart."

Unsnapping my seat belt, I shoulder open the front door. The front end of my car is smashed in. Fear ripples through me.

God, what if the girls are more hurt than I can see?

Don't cry, Harper. Don't cry.

Sirens sound in the distance as I try to open the back door behind me to get them out. Shit. It won't budge. Running around the car to the passenger side, I'm able to squeeze it open and help both of them unbuckle themselves and get out of the car.

"Does anything hurt?" I ask, looking them over, trying to find any signs of injury.

"I'm scared," Sadie tells me again.

"I know, baby. I am too." I press a kiss to her forehead and hold both girls close to me.

"Can we help you and your daughters?" a stranger asks, dropping down next to us.

"I don't know," I tell them.

"The police are here. It was a teenager that hit you," he tells me.

Standing up, there's a police officer talking to a teenage girl that is hysterical. I can only imagine what is going through her head. But she's not my concern.

This is not how I expected the day to go. All I wanted was to take the girls to get ice cream and spend the afternoon with them before Marcus came home. Get dinner and then spend the night with Marcus.

This is a clusterfuck.

I can't imagine his reaction.

"Ma'am, we're going to need you and your daughters to come with us." This comes from a police officer. "The EMTs want to check you over before taking you to the hospital."

"Hospital?" Dread settles in my gut. "Why do we need to go to the hospital?"

"With the airbags deploying, they want to make sure, especially with children involved. And they'll want to check you over for a concussion with your head wound."

"Head wound?"

He nods. "You're bleeding."

"Shit."

Pressing my hand to my forehead, I feel that it's wet.

Whatever I was doing to stop the tears no longer works. They slide down my cheeks as the three of us follow the police officer over to the ambulance.

"Hi girls," the woman greets them. "We're going to check you over and then you're going to get to ride in the ambulance. Have you ever ridden in one before?"

Both girls shake their heads.

"I promise, you won't be scared."

"You're not going to leave us?" Sam turns wide, wet eyes onto me.

"Never."

Not if I can help it.

"Let's get you looked over and then we'll even turn on the lights for you two, okay?"

"Okay." Sadie sniffles, hopping up into the truck. I try to help, but pain shoots through my wrist.

"And we'll make sure your mom is taken care of."

Mom. That's the first time I've ever been called that. And not for the first time, these two were called my daughters.

I want that more than anything.

Both girls tuck themselves into my arms as the EMTs look them over. They are kind and patient with them. It goes a long way to soothing the scared girls I'm holding.

"Is Daddy going to meet us at the hospital?" Sadie asks.

"Yeah. I'll call him."

"Everything looks okay with the girls—"

"Thank God," I breathe.

"Did you lose consciousness at all?" the second EMT asks.

"No."

"Good. They may do a CT scan at the hospital, but they'll be able to go over everything there once we arrive."

"Thank you."

They pack up before heading to the front.

"What about your car?" Sadie asks.

"I think the police will take care of it. Don't you worry about it."

"Can we call Daddy? I want him."

"We'll call him on the way."

Both girls squeeze closer to me as the ambulance starts moving, sirens loud.

Thankfully I had the foresight to grab my phone.

Marcus's phone goes straight to voicemail. Which is going to make the next call even worse when I have to call the team's main switchboard.

I only hope he doesn't hate me by the end of the day.

WELCOME
TO Fabulous
LAS VEGAS
NEVADA

"That was a good practice today, boys." I slap Graham on the helmet as he skates off the ice.

"You know, you have a future in coaching one day," Bode tells me as he skates by.

"What, and deal with people like you?" I laugh. "I don't think so."

"I'm a fucking delight."

"So you say," I tell him.

"Marcus. There's a call for you in my office," Coach Andrews calls out. "Came through the main switchboard."

"What?"

That's odd. I've never gotten a call on the main line before. Well, except once.

That sends panic racing through me. The only time I've gotten a call on the main line was when Jamie was in her accident.

Fuck.

Ignoring every guy coming off the ice, I move as fast as I can to Coach's office. The red light is flashing from his phone. I take a deep breath before picking up the receiver.

"This is Marcus Evans."

"Marcus. This is Nurse Beckett from Nashville Medical—"

"What happened?"

I know I should let her finish, but I can't. Every terrible thought on why she would be calling is flashing through my mind.

"There was an accident. Everyone is okay, but we need you to come down here."

"They're okay?"

What the hell happened?

"Yes, but we'll need you to come down here."

"I'm on my way."

I hang up the phone without another word. Rushing into the locker room, I strip out of my gear and toss it into my locker.

"Everything okay?" Jasper asks.

"The girls were in an accident."

I dig around in my bag for my keys and phone. There's a few missed calls from Harper.

Fuck. I hate that I'm not there with them right now. I can't imagine how scared Sam and Sadie are.

"Are they okay?" Noah asks.

"That's what the nurse said."

I won't breathe a sigh of relief until I lay eyes on all three of them.

"Do you need one of us to drive you down there?" Bode asks.

For the first time in his life, he's serious, and I'm not sure I can handle that right now.

"Thanks, but I'll be okay."

"You sure?" Dax asks.

I nod, finally feeling my keys in my bag. "I'm sure."

I don't waste another minute as I run out of the locker room.

"Keep us posted!" Noah shouts.

By the time I get to my SUV, my hands are shaking. They're okay. The nurse said they were okay.

I don't know if I'll ever get over this feeling…when someone from a hospital calls and you don't know what to expect on the other end of the line.

Deep breaths, Marcus. Deep breaths.

Steadying my hands, I throw the SUV in drive and head toward the medical center. Once I get there, I can figure out what is going on.

Fuck. I'm going to have to call my mom. I haven't had a chance to talk to her about this thing with Harper. And finding out while we're at the hospital?

It's going to go over about as well as a lead balloon.

Cursing late afternoon traffic, I try to get there as fast as I can. Safely, because the last thing I need is to get into another accident on the way there.

I can't imagine how Sam and Sadie are feeling right now. All they know is that their mom and dad died in an accident. That's it.

Hell, I can't imagine what Harper is going through. She loves them, so it has to be eating her up inside. This is not what any of us expected to happen today.

Pulling up to the hospital, I follow signs to the ER and find an empty parking spot. I'm rushing inside, but before I can make it to the desk, a familiar voice is calling out to me.

"Marcus!" Mom's short brown hair is pulled back into a haphazard ponytail. She's wearing a sweatshirt covered with paint. It's like she dropped everything to get here.

"Mom? What are you doing here?"

"The hospital called."

Of course. She's on the girls' emergency contact list. I'm sure they got it from the school if Harper was calling the main switchboard when she couldn't get in touch with me.

"What happened?" I ask, wondering if she knows more.

"I don't know. They're in room four. How's Emma?"

"Emma?"

Mom nods as we follow the signs back toward the room in question. "Wasn't she with the girls? She's usually more careful than this."

"Mom, it was an accident."

"Still. You think she'd take more care."

"Look, Mom. It wasn't Emma."

"Then who's with Sam and Sadie?" Panic is written all over her face. Like I left them with some random stranger off the street.

"Harper."

"Harper? Why does that name sound familiar?" I know the moment it dawns on her who she is. "That Harper? The woman that left you when Jamie and Dan died?"

"Yes."

Her face morphs into anger and rage. "You mean to tell me that's who my granddaughters are with?"

"Look, Mom—"

She holds out a hand to cut me off. "Not now. I need to make sure my grandbabies are okay."

I trail off after her, trying to figure out how to deal with a second crisis. I can hear their voices, and it soothes every worry inside of me.

Mom goes in first, and both girls call out to their Gigi. I'm standing behind them, eyeing Harper.

She looks miserable, ghostly white. There's a small

butterfly bandage on her forehead and a brace around her wrist.

I'm so sorry she mouths to me.

"What in the world is going on here?" Mom asks.

Now that the girls have hugged her, they've made their way over to me. "Are you two okay?"

I push the hair out of their faces. They look fine, as far as I can tell.

"It was scary," Sam tells me, her lip quivering. "We were going to get ice cream after school—"

"Ice cream after school?" Mom huffs. "They're not allowed to have ice cream after school."

"Mom, that's not important right now."

"Harper said it was a special day," Sam continues. "Sadie beat the fifth grader, so we were going to get ice cream to celebrate and then someone crashed into us."

"It was loud. Bags exploded in the car."

"Bags?"

Sadie nods.

"Airbags," Harper confirms. "I'm sorry. I was turning and it was a teenager—"

"It's okay. You're all okay." The last thing I want is for her to worry. It wasn't her fault.

"No, it's not okay!" Mom snaps. "Does she not realize that she has to take better care of Sam and Sadie?"

"Mom!"

"No, she's right." Harper's voice is small. She looks scared and I can't blame her.

"See? She should not be around the girls." Mom's eyes flit between mine and Harper's. The girls are huddled together in my arms. They don't have any clue what's going on, other than Gigi is angry. "How long has this been going on?"

"This is not a discussion we need to be having right now. Not in front of the girls."

It's that moment a nurse walks in. "Everything okay in here?"

"I think we're fine right now."

"No, we are not fine!" Mom snaps. "I want to know what is going on right now."

I look to the nurse. "Are you able to stay with them while I talk to my mother and Harper, please?"

"Sure." She looks hesitant, but I set the girls down.

"I'm going to talk to Gigi for a minute, okay?" They both nod at me.

Mom drops a kiss onto both of their heads and heads out into the hallway, Harper following her.

"I'll be right back, okay? Then we'll go home and I'll make pancakes for dinner."

That earns me the first smile I've seen from them all afternoon. "With chocolate chips?"

I smile at them. "Extra chocolate chips."

"Yes!"

I kiss both of them and by the time I get out there, my mother is seething. Neither woman is speaking to the other.

I don't know if I've ever seen my mom so angry.

"What is she doing here?" Mom nods toward Harper. "Why is she driving Sam and Sadie around and taking them for ice cream?"

"Mom—"

She starts crying, no doubt the emotions of the day catching up with her. I want to console her, but I don't know if I can. Not when Harper is shrinking in on herself.

"The girls are okay," Harper says.

"No thanks to you. What makes you think you have a

right to spend any time with them when you left? You left!"
Mom shouts. It draws a few eyes.

Looking behind me, I see the nurse is reading a book
with the girls. Thank God they're not looking out here.

"That's not what happened, Jane." Harper is shaking
her head.

"I don't want to hear anything else from either of you."
She turns her ire on me. "I don't want her near my granddaughters!"

She goes back into the room without another word.

Harper bursts into tears. "I'm so sorry, Marcus. I'm so
sorry."

"Are you hurt?" I ask, pulling her into my arms.
There's no point in asking if she's okay. No one is okay. Far
from it, in fact.

"I'm fine."

"Then why do you have a brace on your wrist?"

She shakes her head. "It's a sprain. Could have been
worse."

"You were trying to protect them?"

Harper nods, stepping out of my arms. "Of course. I
love them, Marcus. I would do anything to protect them."

"Where are you going?"

Harper keeps walking backward. "You heard your
mom. I don't want to get in the middle of this."

"No, Harper. I'll explain everything to her."

She's shaking her head. "She hates me."

"She doesn't hate you."

"Marcus, c'mon." Harper's voice is watery. "She hates
me, and you know it."

"It was an accident, Harper. It could have happened to
anyone."

"But it happened to me. Look, we need to let things
settle down."

"What are you saying?"

Harper runs forward and gives me a quick kiss. "It means that you need to be with the girls. Take care of them. We'll figure us out later."

"Hey." I try to grab her so she doesn't leave, but she's too fast. "There's nothing to figure out. It's you and me, Harper. You, me, and the girls."

"Until your mom gets on board, I don't know."

She turns and leaves.

As if this day couldn't get any worse, Harper is leaving.

And this time, I don't know if she'll be the one coming back.

Chapter Thirty-One

HARPER

I hate this. It's only been a few days since I saw Marcus and the girls, but I miss them. I miss them more than I ever thought possible.

It's the worst feeling. Some freak accident and his mother found out about us. She kept screaming that I left.

If I wasn't missing all of them so much, I might dig deeper into what she meant. But I don't care right now.

All I want is to be in Marcus's arms, watching Bluey and listening to the girls giggle about their days.

I shouldn't have fallen for them this hard. I should have protected my heart.

How could I possibly do that when Marcus has had it all this time?

It's an endless loop my head is stuck in. With taking a few days off school to recuperate, I don't even have the distraction of teaching to get through.

Just me and my misery.

He's called and texted, but the last thing I want to do is get my hopes up that everything will be okay when he really can't lose any more family.

I don't want to ignore him, but I can't talk to him.

I hate it.

A knock at my front door has me leaping off the couch. My heart falls at seeing Rina standing on the other side.

"Wow. Don't look so happy to see me."

"Sorry." I open the door wider for her to come inside. "I was hoping you'd be someone else."

"Someone named Marcus?" She quirks a brow at me and sets the paper bag in her arms down on the table.

"Wishful thinking, I know."

Rina slips out of her jacket and hangs it on the hook by my front door. "Have you talked to him since the accident?"

I shake my head. "No. He has the girls to worry about."

Rina winces.

"What?" I ask, emptying out the bag to take out containers of Mexican. "What's that face for?"

"I hate to tell you this…"

"Tell me anyway."

I cross my arms and lean my hip against the counter.

"Sam and Sadie are miserable."

"What? Why?" I ask. Anxiety swoops low in my belly. Did something else happen I don't know about?

"Because they miss you. They keep looking into your class to see if you're there."

"I hate this." I bury my face in my hands, trying to stop the emotion that's overcoming me.

Anger. Heartbreak. Tension.

Rina grabs my uninjured wrist and pulls my attention back on her. "Why haven't you called him?"

I worry my bottom lip between my teeth. "I'm scared."

"Why? This is Marcus."

Grabbing the white bag, marked with grease stains from the chips, I open it and stuff one into my mouth.

"I'm scared, okay? His mom kept yelling that I left and that she didn't want me anywhere near her grandchildren. Those girls are his life. Why would he choose me over them?"

"Marcus loves you," Rina points out. "There's no choosing. He wants you *and* the girls. It's not even an option."

My lip quivers and I bite down harder, trying not to let my emotions get the best of me. "But his mom—"

"Honey. Let Marcus deal with his mother. I don't know what's going on there, but based on everything you said, I don't think that's the end of it."

I huff out a laugh. "I wish, but I don't want him to lose any more of his family."

That's what it boils down to.

His sister and brother-in-law.

His father.

Sam and Sadie have known too much loss in their short lives. They adore their grandma. I don't want to be the reason they don't see each other.

Except I don't know how I can live without Marcus. Ever since he came back into my life, I remembered what it was like to love him. To be so swept up in him, that he was the most important thing and I felt like I could take on the world.

"When did love become so hard?" I rest my head on Rina's shoulder.

"It's always been this way. You just have to decide if what you and Marcus have is worth fighting for."

I busy myself with getting plates down to start dishing up our dinner and think about what Rina said. Am I ready to fight for Marcus, or am I willing to lose the person that means more to me than anyone else in the world?

I lost Marcus once.

I don't think I could survive losing him again.

WELCOME
TO
Fabulous
LAS VEGAS
NEVADA

Chapter Thirty-Two

MARCUS

NOAH

Are the girls okay?

MARCUS

They're okay

GRAHAM

Are you okay?

Not so much

BODE

Have you heard from Harper?

No

JASPER

Have you tried calling?

Obviously

And texted

And called and texted again

DAX
Can we help?

I appreciate it, but no

GRAHAM
You sure?

NOAH
We can take the girls for a few hours

I don't know if that would help

Not unless you're Harper

NOAH
Sorry, man

It'll be okay

I lock my phone. I hope if I keep repeating it to myself, things will actually be okay.

It's been almost a week without any word from Harper. Not only do I miss her, but the girls do too.

More so than me, it seems, if their mopey faces at the table have anything to say about it.

"I miss Harper." Sam pushes her mac and cheese around on her plate. "Why isn't she over?"

"She has school things tonight." I drop a kiss onto Sam's head before heading back into the kitchen to grab the green beans I made us. "She'll come over when she's free."

"When will that be?" Sadie whines. "We made her Christmas presents."

I sigh. The holidays are coming up, and I know they'll want to see her. With the accident happening right before holiday break, none of us have been able to talk to her.

"Soon." I set the two plates down in front of them.

"Gigi always says soon is an excuse for people who don't want to come over."

Of course she did.

"I promise. Harper will see you soon."

Dinner is a muted affair. There's no happy chatter of how they spent their day. Nothing about how excited they are for the upcoming holiday.

"Do you maybe want to put up the tree tonight?"

Both girls shrug. Well, I'm not getting much more out of them tonight. Given that it's winter break, I let the girls watch TV until bed, complete with snuggles. With a book before bed, they fall asleep quickly.

I collapse onto the couch, scrubbing my hands over my face. I don't know how much longer I can take this silence from Harper.

She has ignored every single one of my calls and texts. It's not like I can see her at school until classes resume. It's been nothing but silence.

I hate it. I hate that she's avoiding me for something that wasn't her fault. It's gutting me, and made exponentially worse because of the girls.

There's a soft knock at the door. Sitting up, I walk down the hallway to see Harper standing on the front porch through the windows. Her hair is down and she's wearing an oversized Knights sweatshirt and leggings. She spots me and gives me a sad smile.

I don't hesitate in pulling the door open. "Hi."

"Hi."

"What are you doing here?"

Grabbing her hand, I pull her into my arms, holding her there.

"I missed you."

"You could have called, you know," I tell her.

Harper starts crying, based on her shaking. "I'm sorry, Marcus. I'm so sorry."

"You did nothing wrong."

"Yes, I did!" Harper exclaims, pulling back. Tears are streaming down her face. "I hurt them."

I shake my head. "You only hurt them by leaving."

More tears. "But your mom—"

"C'mon." I tuck Harper into my side, then lead us into the living room to reclaim my spot on the couch. This time, with Harper curled up by my side.

"I hate that I put the girls in that situation," Harper whispers into my chest.

I squeeze her closer. "It wasn't your fault."

"But—"

"No. It wasn't your fault. They hit you. Everyone is okay. That's all that matters."

"But your mom—" Harper starts.

I sigh. "Yeah. I don't know what I'm going to do about that."

Harper shifts, resting her chin on my chest to stare at me. "I don't want to come between you and her."

"I might be part of that problem," I confess.

"What do you mean?"

"I never told her I left you back then."

Harper closes her eyes. "So she hates me because she thinks I walked out on you? Of course she does."

"Look." I cup her cheek and wipe away the lingering tears. "It was another mistake in a long line of mistakes I made back then. I was so caught up in my own grief that I never bothered telling the truth."

Harper smiles at me. "I'm not mad. But at least I understand why she hates me so much."

I waggle my finger at her to scoot closer to me, and she slides up my chest. I capture her lips in a warm kiss. It's not heated, but it's perfect. Exactly what I need right now.

"I'll figure something out," I whisper against her lips.

Harper shakes her head. "We can do it together."

"Yeah?"

"You might have been alone before, Marcus, but you're not anymore. It's not just you. It's you and me."

"Don't ever leave us again," I tell her.

"Never. I'm here for you. Always."

"I don't deserve you."

"Well, you must have done something right for us to be back here."

I breathe Harper and her sweet scent in. Her words do more to heal every part of my broken soul than anything else these last few years.

"I love you, Harper. Probably more than I'll ever be able to tell you."

Harper seals her mouth over mine.

"You want to know something?" She traces a finger down the scruff on my jaw. Scruff that I haven't bothered keeping cleaned up because I've been too distraught.

"Tell me," I say.

Harper rests her head on my chest over my heart. "Remember our vows?"

I smile, running my fingers through Harper's hair. "I remember every second of our wedding."

"I never told you, but that night, when I went back to my hotel room, I wrote out what I wanted to say instead of the vows we actually said."

"What, traditional wasn't good enough for you?" I laugh.

"Just didn't really convey everything I felt for you then."

"Then?" I ask.

"Now too."

"So what would you say?" I continue running my fingers through her silky hair. It's calming.

"That I love you with every cell in my body. Every fiber of my being. That there is nothing I wouldn't do for you because of how much I love you. There will never be another person who knows me the way you do. Who loves and cares for me the way you do. How safe I feel when I'm in your arms. And how all I want is to go to bed next to you every night and wake up next to you every morning. If that's all I have in life, I'll have all I need."

"Harper."

She squeezes me close. "You don't have to say anything, Marcus. But however this plays out, I'm not going anywhere."

"Seriously, I don't deserve you."

"Yes, you do." Harper swats at my chest.

"You know, I thought about what I would've said to you too. If we had actually planned a wedding."

Harper laughs and the warmth seeps through my T-shirt. "I mean, you planned it."

"You know what I mean."

"What would you have said?" Harper asks.

"That you're my person. I was in love with you the second I met you. A complete goner. I still remember that day at the pep rally. You looked so beautiful, but everything on the inside made you that much more incredible. I was the luckiest man in the world that I got to be with you. And how I would do everything in my power to make sure you knew how loved you were every day we spent together. Forever and a day."

"Forever and a day."

WELCOME
TO
Fabulous
LAS VEGA
NEVADA

Chapter Thirty-Three

MARCUS

"Harper! You're here!"

Tiny voices startle me awake. Harper is still lying on top of me, eyes wide as she looks at the girls standing in front of us.

Shit. We must have fallen asleep talking on the couch.

"What are you doing here?" Sam asks.

Harper looks at me before sitting up and letting the girls tackle hug her. "I missed you."

"We missed you a lot," Sadie tells her.

"I know, sweetheart." Harper drops a kiss to the top of each of their heads. "I missed you too."

"Did Gigi scare you off?" Sam asks.

"Hey." I sit up and pull Sam onto my lap. "Gigi was mad, but remember what I said?"

She screws her face up, thinking. "That she'll be happy again soon?"

"That's right." I nod. "Now, who wants breakfast?"

"Pancakes?" Sadie asks. "Please?"

I shake my head. "No. Yogurt and fruit this morning."

"Nuts." Sadie follows Sam into the kitchen and pulls out their breakfasts that are premade for them.

"They were hoping they'd get the good stuff since you're here."

Harper laughs. "What a mean dad you are."

"I've got bigger problems than that."

"Like?" Harper asks.

"I need to figure out how to talk to my mom."

Harper takes a deep breath, her lips thinning into a small line. "Do you want me there with you?"

"Yes. Do you really want to?"

She nods. "If we want her to see this is real between us, yes. Just because it's hard, doesn't mean I'm going anywhere."

"I love you."

"I love you too."

"I promise, we'll get through this. You're the best thing in my life, Harper. You and those girls who are probably adding chocolate chips to their yogurt."

Harper peeks behind me and smiles. I know I'm right based on that look.

"All I need to be happy is you three. If my mom can't see that, then that's on her."

"We're doing this together," Harper reiterates.

As if summoned, the front door opens. "Morning, girls."

"We're doing this now?" Harper hisses.

"Crap. I forgot Emma has the day off and she was coming over while I'm at practice."

"Gigi!" Sam yells. "We're having chocolate chips with yogurt for breakfast."

"Okay." I spin on my heel. "We're going to need to have a chat about how many chocolate chips you eat."

Sam looks chagrined as Mom steps into the kitchen.

Her eyes immediately lock on to Harper. I guess this is going to be harder than I thought.

"What is *she* doing here?" Mom spits out.

"I was just leaving." Harper winces and grabs her jacket.

"No," I tell her. There's a demand in my voice. I'm not going to lose Harper again because of my mother. "Mom, you need to know the truth."

Mom crosses her arms, hoisting her bag farther up her shoulder. "That she left when you needed her most?"

Harper scoffs. "That's not what happened."

"One day you were here, then the next you weren't."

"Because—" Harper starts, but I interrupt.

"I left, Mom. Not Harper."

"Stop trying to protect her."

"Sam. Sadie. Go upstairs to your room." I turn to face the girls who have questioning looks on their tiny faces.

"Are we in trouble?" Sadie asks.

"No, Sadie, you're not in trouble. I need to talk to Gigi alone."

"Someone is definitely in trouble," Sam whispers as the two of them head upstairs with their cups of yogurt.

I can't fight the smirk that lands on my face. Of course they think that.

I wait for the sound of their door shutting before I turn toward my mother again. Anger is coming off her in waves. Anger that is directed at Harper when it should be directed at me.

"It's my fault, Mom. Everything that happened when Jamie died? It was my fault."

Mom shakes her head. "It's just like you to take the fall when she left."

"Is that what you think happened?" Harper asks.

"I don't want to hear what you have to say. You aban-doned my son."

"Mom!" I shout. I can't help it. "I left Harper. I didn't think she could take everything that happened and I left. I didn't tell her when Jamie died or when Dad did or when I adopted the girls. Everything that happened is my fault."

"What?"

She looks like someone slapped her. "Why would you tell me she left?"

"Because it was easier. I didn't want to face the fact that I couldn't handle everything that happened and ran away scared."

"I...I..."

Tears are streaming down my mom's face. I should have expected it. My lie has had years to fester and cause her to hate Harper. I figured I would never see Harper again, so why worry about Mom's opinion?

"You didn't leave?" Mom asks Harper.

Harper shakes her head. "Marcus is the love of my life. Nothing could ever make me leave him."

I turn to look at Harper, and a fierce wave of love washes over me. I don't know how I ever left the first time. She is everything to me. The very beat of my heart. "And nothing could ever make me leave her again. Nothing."

Harper walks over to me and takes my hand. "I'm sorry for everything that happened and what you've been through. But I'm not going anywhere. Nothing you or Marcus say is going to drive me away. I love him and those girls more than anything and will do whatever I can to prove that to you."

I press a kiss to Harper's palm, holding it over my heart.

"If you want to hate someone, Mom, hate me. I deserve it."

Harper turns her attention from me to my mom. "Believe me, I hated him for what he did too. Hated him for a lot of years. But that's in the past. We can't change it and can only move forward. I hope you can find it in your heart to forgive me."

"I can't believe you lied, Marcus." Mom shakes her head at me.

"I'm sorry, Mom. I know I caused you a lot of pain by not telling you the truth."

"But why? Why wouldn't you tell me?"

I shrug a shoulder. "I hated myself for walking out. Losing Dad and Jamie? I'd rather you didn't hate me for what I did too. Over the years, it just got easier to keep up the lie."

Mom covers her mouth with her hand. "This is a lot for me to take in right now. I need some time to digest all of this."

The fact that she's contrite bodes well for us. I don't dare let the seed of hope plant itself inside of me. I don't want it to be stomped out before it has a chance to grow.

"Take your time," Harper tells her. "I'm going to head out and let you two talk before you leave, okay?"

I nod. "I love you." I give her a quick peck, then she's out the door.

Mom walks over and pats my cheek. "I could wring your neck, son."

I give her a sympathetic smile. "I know."

"Why didn't you tell me any of this?"

"I never meant to keep lying to you, but I never thought I'd get a second chance with Harper."

"I should have known you two would have a second chance. You loved her like your father loved me."

I smile at her. "Dad always did say you were the one great love of his life."

Mom's brown eyes grow wet again. "I miss that man every day."

"I know. It's how I felt about Harper. Missing her."

Pressing onto her toes, Mom kisses my cheek. "Then don't let her go. Don't let anyone get in the way between the two of you. Not even your egos."

"I won't, trust me. I'm not letting Harper go for anything."

"Good. Maybe once the girls get home from visiting Dan's parents, we can all get together?"

"I'm sure she'd like that," I tell her.

"I can get to know her again. Hear what's been going on in her life the last few years."

It's the best I could have hoped for today.

"Can we come out yet?" Sam calls from upstairs.

"Come on down."

Their feet thunder down the stairs.

"Did Harper leave?" Sadie asks. "I wanted to see her again."

"She'll be back tomorrow, okay?" I tell her.

"She's not in trouble?" Sam asks.

"No," Mom answers. "Harper isn't in trouble. No one is in trouble."

"You sounded mad," Sam states, Sadie nodding along with her.

"No one is mad," I tell them. "We're all fine."

Mom looks at me in agreement.

Yeah, everything is going to be just fine.

Chapter Thirty-Four

HARPER

"I'm nervous." I shake out my hands, not for the first time tonight.

"Why?" Marcus steps behind me, tugging me into his arms.

"Because, I want your mom to like me."

It's the first time we're all getting together since Marcus confessed the truth to her. They spent the holidays together before the girls went to visit their grandparents in Washington. She volunteered to travel with them, so she's bringing them home tonight.

I'm hoping the small present I have for Jane will help smooth the bumpy road we have ahead of us.

"I think I might need to get in her good graces more than you."

I laugh. "You're her son. She'll eventually get over it."

"The woman can hold a grudge. I hope it's not a trait the girls get."

"Nah. They have you. I'm not worried."

Warmth blooms in my chest. This is everything I ever wanted in life. Marcus. A family. It's everything I never dreamed I could get. Instead of the accident putting a wedge between me and Marcus, it only brought us closer together.

"We're home!" Sam and Sadie's voices ring out through the house.

Marcus and I scurry around the island to greet the girls. Bright and happy faces meet us, cheeks pink from the cold.

"Daddy! Harper!"

Sadie jumps into my waiting arms as Sam tackles Marcus around the legs.

"I missed you," I tell Sadie.

"I missed you too. But I played a lot of chess with Nana."

"You did? Did you win?" I ask her.

She nods. "Yes. Nana and Papa aren't very good."

I hug Sadie to me, missing this girl more than I thought. "Maybe you can beat me tonight."

"Deal."

Sadie wiggles out of my arms before she goes to hug Marcus. I bend down to hug Sam. "I missed you too, sweetheart."

"We got you a present from Seattle."

"You're so sweet."

"And look." Sam smiles at me. "I lost another tooth."

"Did the tooth fairy come?"

She nods. "I got five dollars."

"Five dollars?" Marcus interjects. "The tooth fairy is very generous."

"That's what I said," Jane laughs.

"Thanks for traveling with them, Mom," Marcus tells her.

"I know you had practice. I liked getting the time."

Jane turns her attention to me, and I do my best not to

squirm. The smile on her face is warm, but I'm still wary. I want her to like me for me and not only because Marcus loves me.

"Dinner is ready if you're hungry," I tell them.

"What are we having?" Sadie asks, as Marcus takes the girls' backpacks and coats.

"Your favorite." I take Sam's hand and lead her into the kitchen.

"Spaghetti!" She runs over to the table and climbs into her seat. The table is set with dishes covered and waiting to be eaten.

"This looks great," Jane tells me. "Thanks for inviting me."

"We're glad you could stay."

Marcus smiles at me as we all take our seats.

"Marcus tells me you're a teacher at the girls' school?" Jane asks, dishing out spaghetti to the girls as I pass over the salad bowl.

"I am. I taught first grade, but moved to second grade and I love it."

"School is my favorite," Sadie chirps.

I don't miss the eye roll Sam gives her. I know Sam isn't the biggest fan of school, but I'm hoping that might change with me around.

Sam and Sadie tell us all about their trip with their grandparents while we eat our dinner.

"They even took us to see their neighbor's puppy," Sam tells us. "They said you should get us a dog."

"Of course they did. There will be no dog." Marcus gives the girls a pointed look.

"But why not? We'll take care of him." Sadie has a pleading look on her face.

"Why don't you two go play with some of your new Christmas gifts?" Marcus tells them, more than asking.

"Do we get dessert after?" Sam asks.

I nod. "Yes. I made cheesecake for everyone."

Sam gives me a kiss on the cheek before running after Sadie. Having helped Marcus move all their new toys into their playroom, I know they'll be occupied for hours.

"You won't be able to dodge that for much longer," I tell Marcus.

"I know. Maybe for their birthday next summer."

"Good plan," Jane says. "Dinner was wonderful."

"All Marcus. I can bake, but Marcus is the chef."

She smiles back at me. "A perfect couple then."

Marcus peeks over at me and sends a wink my way.

"I have a present for you."

"You didn't have to do that." Jane waves me off.

"I know, but I wanted you to have it."

I walk over to the Christmas tree to grab the small box that I set under it so I wouldn't forget it. Placing it in her hand, I watch as she unwraps it.

"Oh, Harper."

She fingers the antique locket that I found when Rina and I went to a Christmas market when Marcus was out of town. I knew it would be perfect the minute I found it.

On one side is a picture of Jamie and her husband with Marcus, Sam, and Sadie on the other.

"We'll need to update this photo." She points to the one of Marcus and the girls.

"Oh." My heart drops. I really thought she would like this.

"We'll need one of all five of us."

"Really?"

She nods. "I'll need one of my entire family together."

Standing, I move around the table to pull her into a hug. Her eyes are wet, just like mine. "Thank you for this,

Harper. I don't deserve your kindness. After everything I said—"

"No." I shake my head. "That's all behind us. We're moving forward. I love Marcus and the girls, and I want us all to be a family."

Jane pats my cheeks, wiping my eyes. "I would like that very much. But you know what that means?"

"Don't say it, Mom," Marcus groans from behind me.

"What is it?" I look between the two of them.

"Grandbabies. I want lots and lots of grandbabies."

"You already have two, Mom."

"What?" She grabs her plate and carries it into the kitchen. "I want to spoil more. So get on it."

More groaning from Marcus as he tugs me down into his lap. "Did you encourage this idea?"

"I had nothing to do with it." I drape an arm around his shoulders. "But you know I won't mind trying."

That perks him up. "Are we already having the kids discussion?"

I whisper in his ear, "We're already married."

"Fair point. I kind of like this idea."

"Really?" I ask. "You want more kids?"

"Are you having a baby?" Sam asks.

"Fuck me," Marcus mutters, burying his face in my arm. "They had to come in now."

"We're not having a baby."

"You're not?" Sadie looks sad at this news.

"Do you want a baby brother or sister?" I ask them.

"Yes!" they answer in unison.

"I want a baby sister," Sam tells me.

"Me too," Sadie agrees.

"Do you want a baby sibling or a puppy?" Marcus asks them.

"Puppy!"

"Baby!"

Each of them gives a different answer that has the three adults in the room laughing.

"Well, we're not getting both," Marcus says.

"We can get a puppy later," Sadie tells Sam. "I want a baby sister."

"I don't want a baby bother," Sam confirms. "Boys are smelly."

"Hey! I'm not smelly," Marcus tells them.

"After hockey you are," Sam says. "Really smelly."

"Okay. I'm more likely to get you a puppy instead of a baby."

"Really?" Wide, hopeful eyes look back at us.

"I'll talk to your dad about it," I tell them.

"We're getting a puppy!" they chant around the living room.

"You sure you're ready for life with these two?" Marcus asks.

Cupping his cheeks, I kiss him. Soft and sweet. "Yeah, Marcus. I want this life with all three of you."

"Then get ready for chaos."

"I can't wait."

"Girls, no more snacks until lunch, okay?"

"Really, Mom?" Sam groans. "But I'm hungry."

I shake my head at her. The minute she turned nine last year, the sass came. "Uncle Bode is finishing up the hot dogs soon, sweetheart, okay? Drink some water and go play with Jamie."

"Fine."

She stomps away, before spotting her friends and running into the melee.

"You know she'll be back up here in a few minutes, right?" Marcus tells me, pulling me down onto his lap.

The backyard is filled to the brim with people to celebrate a successful season for the Knights. They made it all the way to the conference finals, and they were one win away from going to the Stanley Cup finals. And that's reason enough to celebrate—how far this team has come.

"I can at least try to hold the girls off. They've been eating nothing but chips and candy all afternoon. I do not want to deal with sick kiddos tonight."

"You know they'll be monsters after they crash from all this sugar." Marcus presses a kiss to my neck.

"Maybe that means they'll go to bed early." I waggle my eyebrows at my husband, pushing my sunglasses onto the top of my head.

"Don't go giving me any ideas that you can't make good on right now, Harper."

"Oh, I plan to make good on every one of them."

Marcus groans. "Now you're just teasing."

I press a warm kiss to his lips. "You make it easy, oh sexy husband of mine."

"You're so mean."

I smile down at him. "You love it."

"I don't know why I do."

"You can't think of one reason?" I wiggle my hips on top of his lap.

"Right now? Not a one." Marcus nips at my ear. "Not one single reason why I love you comes to mind."

"Hmm, well. I can't wait to show you all the reasons I love you later."

Marcus groans as I hear the sounds of a happy baby.

"Do I need to separate you two?" Noah drops into the chair across from us, Jamie in his arms.

"No." I hold my arms out for my son and he reaches for me immediately. "How's my baby boy?"

Not long after we got married, well, renewed our vows, I got pregnant. We weren't expecting it that soon, but Jamie might be the most doted-on member of our family.

The girls adore him. Marcus loves showing him off to every person he meets. Gigi spoils him. Me? I take pride in the fact that I'm my son's favorite person.

Mama's boy through and through.

"I don't know how Jamie has so much energy. I'm

exhausted," Noah says. "I gave him a freezie pop and after running around, I'm ready for a nap."

"Aww. Uncle Noah can't hang," Marcus says, rubbing a finger over Jamie's chubby cheek.

A bright smile lights up his face. Two front teeth are jutting out from his bottom gum with another one popping down from the top. It's the cutest smile in the world.

"I'll put him down for a nap before lunch."

"I set his pack and play up in Bode's office," Marcus tells me.

"Thanks." I kiss his lips.

Bode's house is an ode to modern architecture. It fits him to a T. Stark white walls with black fixtures and furniture that doesn't look welcoming. His office is about the only room in the entire house that looks lived in.

Photos of him playing decorate the walls as well as old jerseys from his college days. By the time I'm laying him down, Jamie is sucking on his thumb, falling right to sleep.

With Bode having a pool and a sprawling backyard, he hosts get-togethers for the team often. Everyone loves it—especially the kids.

Turning on the baby monitor, I head back outside where all of the guys are hanging around the food table. The girls already have hot dogs on their plates and are scarfing them down.

"Slowly, please. No choking."

"Uncle Bode said we can play with his giant chess set when we're done." Sadie is bouncing with excitement.

"Are you sure, Bode?" I ask, grabbing my own hot dog.

"Eh. Who else is going to use it? I don't play chess."

"That's because I beat him," Sadie gloats.

"That's mean, tiny Evans." Bode feigns hurt. "I'll take you on after lunch."

"Twenty bucks says I win," Sadie bets.

"Don't take that bet, Bode," Marcus tells him. "You're going to lose."

"Oh no. I'll take you on." Bode walks over and shakes Sadie's hand.

"My sister is going to beat you," Sam tells him, matter-of-factly.

Sadie never holds back, and Bode never lets her win. None of us do. Sadie has taken on every one of these guys and beat them all. I'm so proud of my girl.

"I always love watching Sadie kick your ass, Bode," Marcus says.

"You guys are mean, especially considering I invited everyone here."

"We like your pool," Noah deadpans.

"See if I invite you over again." Bode pulls his sunglasses down and grabs Noah's drink before heading back to the pool. But before he gets far, a woman with a car seat carrier rounds the house into the yard.

"Excuse me. Is there a Bode Adams here?"

"That's me." Bode holds out his hand.

"I'm Miss Mitchell from the Tennessee Department of Children's Services."

"Why are you here?" Bode looks confused. "I don't have any kids."

"Oh shit," Marcus whispers next to me, looking down into the car seat.

"I've been trying to get ahold of you for a few weeks now and was told you'd be here," the older woman says. She holds out a stack of papers to Bode, who doesn't take them. "This is your son."

"I'm sorry, what?"

"Your son."

"What the fuck?"

Want more Marcus and Harper? Grab their bonus
scene now!

Need Bode's book NOW? The Playmaker is coming May
2. Preorder now!

Bonus Scene

Timeline note: this takes place two months after the end of chapter 34, so before the epilogue

"Are you ready?" Angie asks, adjusting the snoozing baby in her arms.

I laugh, running a finger over her daughter's cheek. "You know we're already married, right?"

Angie shrugs a shoulder, swaying from side to side. I don't even think she realizes she's doing it. "You're still getting 'married.' It's a big deal."

I smile at her before pulling her in for a one-armed hug. "I'm ready. And I'm glad you were able to make it."

Angie pecks me on the cheek. "Had to come to one of your weddings."

I laugh. "Well, this will be the last. Unless we decide to renew our vows again down the road."

"It'd be just like you two to do that," Rina agrees.

I love that two of my favorite people are here with me

today. Grabbing my lip gloss from the dresser, I swipe one last coat over my lips. "I would marry Marcus one hundred times over if it means I get to spend every day with him."

I give myself one last look in the small mirror. My makeup is immaculate today, and my hair is pinned back in a neat bun with a few tendrils falling down around my face.

"You look stunning, Harper," Rina says.

I didn't want anything fancy for today. Thin straps hold up the white satin material of my dress. It gathers at my hip before flowing around my legs. The slit up the leg will be the perfect tease for Marcus.

"Thanks." Spinning on my heel to see my friends, I find tears are running down Angie's face. "What's wrong? Today is a happy day."

"I know it is." Angie waves a hand in front of her face, trying to dry her eyes. "I fully blame Cam for making me so emotional."

"It only gets worse," Rina says. "The more kids you have, the more emotions you get."

Angie gives her a watery laugh. "Oh good. Something to look forward to."

There's a knock at the bedroom door before it bursts open. "Are you ready, Mom? Daddy sent us to make sure you're ready. He said five minutes."

Mom.

It still makes me want to cry every time I hear the girls call me that. When we told them that we were going to renew our vows, I was nervous. I love them, but didn't know how they would feel with me being around all the time. After a few anxious moments of them whispering, they asked if they could call me Mom and said that their heavenly mommy would be okay with it.

I didn't even pretend to hold it together when I told them they could and wrapped them in my arms.

I love these two like they're my own. I only wish Jamie could be here to see what beautiful girls they've grown into.

"I'm ready, Sadie. How's Dad?"

Sam giggles next to her. "He keeps walking around."

I smile. "He's nervous."

"That's why he sent us to come get you," Sadie says.

Angie laughs. "C'mon. We can't keep him waiting."

"One minute." I crook my finger at the girls. "I have something for you two."

"What is it?" Sam's eyes light up.

Reaching into the top drawer of my dresser, I feel the soft velvet of the necklace boxes and pull both out. "Open it and find out."

Each box holds a silver necklace with three interlocked hearts on its cushion. "One heart for each of your moms, and one for you. This way, you know that we're always with you."

"It's so pretty," Sadie tells me. Her smile—complete with a missing tooth—is huge. "I love it."

"Can we wear them now?" Sam asks.

"Of course. Let me help you."

Sweeping their hair off their necks, I fasten each necklace. Both girls are wearing light pink dresses. Sam's has sequins covering hers with a tulle skirt and Sadie's is a plain, sleeveless dress with a heart pattern covering it.

"I love you girls. You look so beautiful."

"We love you too."

I give them each a kiss on the cheek before grabbing their hands and heading downstairs.

When we decided to renew our vows, we wanted it to be something small with the people we love most in the world. And what better spot to have it than our backyard?

A small group is waiting out on the back deck. The minute I spot them, nerves gather in my belly. The girls run ahead to meet everyone.

My breath catches as I spot him. Marcus stands a head taller than everyone. He looks perfect in his gray suit. His tie matches the girls' dresses.

I can't believe this man is mine.

"Took you long enough." A sexy smirk is playing on his lips the minute I step outside.

"Had to look good for my husband-to-be."

Marcus wraps his arms around my waist and pulls me flush against him. "You could have worn a paper bag, Harper, and you would still look gorgeous."

I link my fingers behind his neck, playing with the soft hairs. "How do I look in my dress then?"

Marcus leans close, his warm breath ghosting the shell of my ear. "Stunning. But it will look even better on the floor tonight."

I dig my fingertips into his neck. "You think you're getting lucky tonight?"

"I know I'm getting lucky tonight."

"Hmm, maybe," I tease.

"C'mon, you two. It's time to go," someone shouts from behind us.

"Ready to get married?" Marcus asks. Nothing but love is shining out of his eyes.

"We're already married," I correct.

"Fine. Married again."

I give him a chaste kiss. "I'd marry you every single day if I had the chance."

Marcus steals one more kiss before grabbing my hand and leading the way where a small pergola is set up with flowers wrapped around each column. It's simple, but perfect for us.

Everyone is already waiting for us under the old oak tree.

"You two ready?" our officiant asks. It's not anyone we know, but someone we found to perform the quick ceremony.

"Yes!" the girls respond. "Our mom and dad are getting married."

"Well then,"—she smiles at Sam and Sadie—"let's get started."

Everyone crowds behind us as Marcus and I move toward the front. She talks about marriage and two people loving each other.

It's not the first time I've heard this, but hopefully will be the last. Marcus must be thinking the same thing based on the smirk on his face.

"Now, I believe you two have written your own vows. Marcus, would you like to start?"

He nods, squeezing my hands as he brushes his thumb over my knuckles. "Harper, the last time we stood up like this, we promised to love and support one another. I didn't believe in that love enough. I never should have doubted you. You have shown me that your love knows no bounds. I will never doubt you again. I will show up for you every day like you do for me. For Sam and Sadie. I thought our life together was over when I left you, but I should have known our love could survive anything. Even if I didn't know it at the time. Thank you for loving me. For supporting me. For being the only person in the world that could love me the way you do."

Tears are rolling down my face. Hope and love are blooming in my chest. Because I know—this time—we'll be together forever.

"Harper, would you like to say a few words to Marcus?"

I smile at her, taking a deep breath to steady myself. "Marcus, I never believed in soulmates. When we first got married, I loved you. You were my person. No matter what happened, I turned to you. But when the years passed and you weren't there, that love never faded. When you came back into my life, I knew you were my soulmate. Even if we were both a little damaged. There's no other way to describe why we found one another. Two souls so connected that they can only be together. A tether that might have stretched thin, but never broke. You stole my heart all those years ago, and I know you will guard it with everything you are. I promise to do the same to yours. To love you and our family with everything I have. Because you, Sam, and Sadie are it for me. You, Marcus Evans, are my soulmate. I love you."

Marcus is wiping tears from his face. Sniffles from our family can be heard. We exchange our rings—a white gold band with diamonds for me and a titanium one for Marcus.

"I now pronounce you husband and wife. You may kiss your bride."

"Hell yeah!" Marcus shouts before sweeping me into his arms and laying one on me. It's wet from our tears, but perfect. The best kiss of my life. Because it seals the love we have for one another.

It's short and sweet because the girls wrap their arms around us as everyone comes to hug us. I don't know if I've ever been surrounded by so much love.

"I love you," Marcus tells me.

I beam back at him. The man I love with every cell in my body, who has given me everything I have ever wanted in my life.

"I love you. Forever and a day."

. . .

NEED BODE'S BOOK NOW? The Playmaker is coming May 2. Preorder now!

Author's Note

BOOK TWENTY-FOUR IS OUT IN THE WORLD!

Y'all. I cannot even begin to tell you how much I love Marcus and Harper's story. When I started writing Best Kept Secret, Marcus and Harper were going to ride off into the sunset. I don't know when it came to me, but their story hit me like a stroke of lightning. I HAD to write it! I loved how it came together and I hope you loved it as much as I did.

Thank you to Tina, Maria, Lily, Swati, and Claire for being some of my favorite people in the book world. I love that I can bounce the craziest of ideas off of you and you never tell me I can't do it. I can't wait to see what this year brings!

To all the readers out there…thank you for reading my books and letting me write books that I love! Your excitement for them keeps me going on the hard days. To the Silver Society, my Street and Influencer teams…thank you for shouting about my books! You're why I get to do what I do.

<3 Emily

Sideline Infraction

Illegal Contact

The Big Game

Moose Falls, Maine

Merry in Moose Falls

A Grump in Moose Falls

Standalones

Off the Deep End

The Highland Escape

Power Pose

Love Pucked - a sapphic hockey romance, coming late 2025

The Ainsworth Royals

Royal Reckoning

Reckless Royal

Royal Relations

Royal Roots

The Love Abroad Series

An Icy Infatuation

A French Fling

A Sydney Surprise

About the Author

After winning a Young Author's Award in second grade, Emily Silver was destined to be a writer. She loves writing inclusive stories, with strong heroines and the swoony men who fall for them.

A lover of all things romance, Emily started writing books set in her favorite places around the world. As an avid traveler, she's been to all seven continents and sailed around the globe.

When she's not writing, Emily can be found sipping cocktails on her porch, reading all the romance she can get her hands on and planning her next big adventure!

Find her on social media to stay up to date on all her adventures and upcoming releases!

www.ingramcontent.com/pod-product-compliance
Lightning Source LLC
Chambersburg PA
CBHW061340310726
48974CB00001B/134